The Islands

ALSO BY DIONNE IRVING

Quint

The Islands

Stories

———————

DIONNE IRVING

Catapult
New York

First Catapult edition: 2022

Versions of these stories have appeared in *Story Magazine, New Flash Fiction Review, New Delta Review, Crab Orchard Review, Terminus Magazine,* and *The Missouri Review.*

ISBN: 978-1-64622-066-3

Library of Congress Control Number: 2021949764

Cover design by Nicole Caputo
Book design by Wah-Ming Chang

Catapult
New York, NY
books.catapult.co

Printed in the United States of America

1 3 5 7 9 10 8 6 4 2

For Ellison, Maxine, and George.
My three favorite Jamaicans.

No man is an island,
Entire of itself;
Every man is a piece of the continent,
A part of the main.

JOHN DONNE
"Meditation 17"

—————

We're gonna help our people, help them right;
Oh, Lord, help us tonight!
Cast away that evil spell;
Throw some water in the well,
And smile!

BOB MARLEY
"Smile Jamaica"

Contents

The Islands

Florida Lives

IN HINDSIGHT, I can see now that we never should
have left San Francisco. My husband was unemployed,
and I was working only part-time, teaching at a private elementary school: making papier-mâché, making
eyes at the principal. We'd spent seven years racking up
credit card debt and taking jobs we hated. We played
the lottery and blew the last of our savings on a Danish
modern couch. We laughed, we cried. We were in our
thirties, childless, broke, on the verge of cliché.

Until the call from a fledgling fern nursery arrived,
looking for someone, anyone, willing to market their
little company, willing to start over in Florida, reloca-
tion expenses included. Before we left, there was a party
in our honor. Family, friends (old and new), lovers, ene-
mies, co-workers. It was at a Thai restaurant in the Ten-
derloin, part charming teak tables, part roaches in the

bathroom. At a table set for twenty, we were toasted amid hot platters of pad thai and lemongrass chicken and so much wine.

San Francisco and so many of the people there were a part of the story of me and my husband. The past imperfect. The verb we would conjugate ourselves out of by putting the distance of a continent between us and it. Us and them. We could pretend that the things that made us different from each other in San Francisco— mine, an immigrant's understanding of the world; and his, a legacy of the W. E. B. Du Bois idea of the Talented Tenth—that idea that a handful of Blacks would use art and education to lead the rest to salvation, use their privilege to remake Black life in America—didn't actually matter all that much.

In the dim lighting of the restaurant, everyone looked a little nostalgic, and a little relieved. And when anyone asked us, *Why Florida?* they'd wrinkled their noses, looks of disgust telegraphing images of six-foot-long alligators, bath-salt-eating criminals, and that giant mouse presiding over his southern fiefdom of plastic and capitalism. I responded: *Did you know that Apopka, Florida, is the international foliage capital of the world?* As if that explained it. As if anything could.

The two of us drank down our doubts. And then we drank a bit more. And with the booze and good vibes coursing through us, we messed around in the back of a taxi on the way home, like we used to, when we first met. This was how we started our Florida lives.

Our rented house in Apopka was walking distance from a swamp, freeway adjacent, perfect. Florida smelled like Jamaica—like what I remembered of it. A mixture of rain-soaked earth and blooming flowers. In Florida we were credit poor and cash rich again. Florida was like living in a giant discount store. Florida with its miles of air-conditioned shopping plazas, its preponderance of drive-thru liquor stores, and the rent that made it seem like you were living almost for free. In Florida we made less money, but it went so much further. San Francisco broke was Central Florida middle class and we could live like the bougie frauds we always wanted to be. Here, our dinners were feasts: expensive cheeses, twenty-five-dollar bottles of wine, meat without the bright orange *Reduced for Quick Sale* sticker. Oh, the luxury!

In Florida, I played the part of the wife that my dark-skinned mother-in-law had always imagined: the light-skinned daughter-in-law there to inject some good hair into their family's genetic pool. To give the family that taste of the American Dream that all of their hard work and private schools could not.

In the Great Migration his people had gone west, not north from the American South, starting from Alabama. Their California lives were going to be better than those of their kinfolk who went to Chicago. Their American Dream would be glamorous, their version of new Black America would be envied. The transformation completed with that husband of mine, with his polo shirts, his affinity for German cars, his confusion that not everyone had a trust fund, a summer home, parents to call when you were in a jam. Their plan—as I understood it—meant a life that would bring them close to white. Or closer at least. A plan to make slavery a distant memory. A plan not unlike my Jamaican family's own. That I was light-skinned made the idea of the imagined future seem closer. I would give them the light-skinned grandkids who would have access to private clubs, and better schools, and all the privileges of near whiteness that his family could imagine and those that they couldn't.

In Florida, I stayed home and played around with complicated recipes. My Jamaican mother's cow tongue soup and escovitch fish, his mother's macaroni and meat loaf! Love: American fusion–style. We each gained five pounds. We stuck my husband's first paycheck on the refrigerator with a flourish. We bought more things we didn't need (teacup-sized succulents, an electric wine opener) and hung our new drapes—hot pink and cream—with aplomb.

In the evenings we dragged plastic beach chairs out onto the front lawn and watched a colony of bats circle our house at sunset. We watched them arc upward and wend their way in slow, concentric circles above the neighborhood. We toasted them with plastic cups, celebrating our escape. We were going to create a new version of Black millennial marriage. Black poverty chic. Reverse aspirational. We were going to use the mass of land between us and our California lives to evaporate what had been so messy and let the spell of Florida take hold.

Secretly, I loved: spreading out across the bed after my husband left for work, devouring whole boxes of hot and sticky donuts, and knowing that no one here knew us.

Secretly, I hated: my husband's colleagues at the fern nursery and their questions—*You tan so well, aren't you exotic looking? How come you're so much lighter than him?* and *Where did you say your family's from?*

In Florida we were the same, and not the same. We were a young Black married couple. We were a unit. But I couldn't understand the rhythms of what it meant to be Black in the most American of American places. But my husband did. He knew what it meant to live in a neighborhood where we were the only Black family. He knew what it meant that his boss spoke of his hard work as if it were a novelty, knew how to smile when someone asked if you knew their Black acquaintance from high school or college, understood that he needed to be well dressed at the grocery store, at the post office, at the car wash. These things were second nature.

And me? I tried to pretend to understand. Me? I was taking lessons about how to be Black in the American South. How to be Black in Florida. How to sublimate yourself, even when it felt unnatural.

Together, we loved: our new bicycles, buying wine in the grocery store, the plush seats of our new SUV, the easy life, the suburban life.

Together, we hated: the way Florida always made you feel like you were standing in a damp basement, the word *irregardless*, and our neighbors. Our neighbors. Oh, we hated them most of all.

Even before we met them, we knew they weren't the kind of people we wanted to know. Yellow grass, cartoon-print bedsheets in the front window instead of curtains, and cigarette butts like bread crumbs from their carport to their patio. We had lived in the house only for a week when they rang our doorbell in three short, staccato bursts. I peered at them through the peephole for a beat too long.

My husband hadn't learned to be anything but casually suspicious of people. Like I said, he wasn't Jamaican. He told me to open the door; they weren't there to hurt us or make our lives more difficult. "It's a couple," he said. "They're being neighborly."

I opened the door, using one arm to close off the

space between my body and the doorframe, my other hand on my hip, not opening the door all the way. They introduced themselves as Crystal and Ricky Fletcher. I didn't offer up our names. But my husband, oh my husband, so trusting, hovered behind me in the brown-and-orange Formica-tiled hall of our rented home and not only invited them in but invited them to sit on our blue velvet chesterfield sofa—*my* blue chesterfield sofa—in dirty cutoff shorts. He was like that—he trusted all people to a fault. My mother said it was all the time he'd spent at private school. "Too much tennis camp," she said, "and not enough Jesus." For her, not enough religion was a straight path both to hell and to people like the Fletchers. Maybe those were the same thing.

Crystal noticed right away how I looked at her. I'd never been good at hiding what I felt.

"I'm so sorry," she said. "We've been working in the yard all day. I usually dress much nicer than this."

It was a twofer. That yard hadn't been touched in at least three months, and Crystal's T-shirt: *I put the "ho" in hotel.*

In Jamaica, you learned to back away from people like Crystal. My parents hadn't raised me in America to socialize with Crystals. They had come to America to make sure I met people like my husband. Black people with more education than sense. They had come to America to keep me away from places like Apopka. But

I hadn't learned—ever—to save a penny for every penny you spent, and here I was in Florida, after all, stacks of credit card bills piled on a table in the front hall and Crystal on my sofa showing me all the ways I'd failed.

I offered our neighbors wine, which they guzzled greedily. Ricky wiped his mouth with the back of his hand and pushed his glass forward for me to pour him a second.

Did you know that Lake Apopka is the fourth-largest lake in the continental United States? (It actually isn't.) Did you know it is teeming with bass? (I wasn't ever going to find out.) Ricky knew. And he also knew about the best spots in the lake to find those bass, and about local real estate, and the value of a dollar. When we got around to the subject of jobs, Ricky explained that he worked as a handyman for the Arabs (which he pronounced *Ay-rabs*) who owned the HoJo on Main Street. He looked at me a little funny when he said it, like perhaps he was trying to figure out if I was one of them.

"They're the good kind," he said finally, holding out his empty glass for a third refill. "Not like the terrorist kind. Man, Patel even jump-started my car when the battery died last week."

"Hells yeah," Crystal echoed. "They're good people."

I inched closer to my husband on the love seat and farther away from Ricky's mud-caked boots. I squeezed my husband's arm to make sure he saw the boots, the ones leaving flakes of mud on our floor. But he pulled away from me, and so I asked Crystal what she did for work.

"Oh, I'm between things right now," she said, twirling a limp strand of dirty-blond hair around her finger. "But I was working as a medical assistant in my last job. Got to wear scrubs and everything."

The idea of Crystal being allowed to do anything medical terrified me. I made an excuse about starting dinner. There was an awkward pause, where I should have asked them to stay, but instead smiled graciously and took their glasses. In the kitchen I performed the Caribbean magic my mother taught me to get rid of unwanted company, turning a broom upside down and sprinkling salt on it. It was either completely effective or wishful thinking, but moments later, with relief, I heard the click of the front door.

As they passed by the kitchen window—they couldn't see me behind the thick crepe paper blinds—I heard Ricky murmur, "I can see he's Black, but what is *she*?"

"I'm not sure," Crystal responded. "I can't tell. It's so hard to tell these days."

And what was I, really? I wondered as I leaned over the sink, trying to hear the rest of the conversation. But by then they were too far away and anything else I might have heard was muffled when my husband turned on the TV in the next room.

"They seemed nice," my husband called out.

Nice. The word hung limply in the air between us. It meant everything and nothing. It was just what I'd said about him, back when he was the cute guy in the next apartment. Not the man I was going to marry. Not the man I did marry.

I mixed a vodka tonic and came into the living room.

"They're horrible people," I said, sitting next to him on the couch. "The worst kind."

"What kind is that? They seemed all right to me."

I searched for a diplomatic way to say *trashy.* This was one of our San Francisco problems, the ways my husband accused me of snobbery. So I didn't respond and I gulped the drink instead.

"And you," my husband said, prodding me ever so slightly in the rib. "I thought you were going to make dinner."

We sat there and drank vodka tonics until the street went dark, until the infomercials came on, until we fell into drunken, ugly sleep, arms akimbo, and mouths open.

But I was right, and it didn't take long for my husband to hate them, too. We heard their fights almost daily. Especially in the early-morning hours, when the quiet drinkers have passed out and the belligerent ones are gearing up for a fight, and then it was *Fuck you!* and *Nah, fuck you!*

We did not fight like this. We fought like white people on TV. We whispered things under our breath. We exchanged terse statements on Post-it notes throughout the house like a kind of study guide to the arguments we were having. We did drink. We did fight. We did *not* drink *and* fight. Especially not in this Florida Life. Certainly not in this picture of ourselves that we were working so hard to maintain.

The Fletchers' fights usually ended with Ricky sitting in his truck with the windows rolled down listening to Metallica's *Master of Puppets*. After "Welcome Home" there was a pause while he flipped the cassette over in the tape deck, and then we all heard the rest of the album. Ricky listened to the album once all the way through if it was a small fight. But when things were really bad, when we heard the crash of plates or glasses, he would listen to it three or four times before heading back into the house. After nights like that, we'd see them heading off to work or getting the mail, and they'd smile at us innocently, as though the night had been devoid of shrieks and cries. And we hated them for that, too. The loud way they railed at each other, the way they could pretend we weren't all hearing. Every time, I would remember what my mother always said about screaming like a fishwife in the market. That was not going to be me. No sir.

We hated them more when they started borrowing

things we knew they had no possibility of returning: cigarettes, rubber bands, ice cubes, Cokes, flour. The kinds of things that require a trip to the store to replace. They never went to the store. Other than greasy paper sacks of fast food, I never saw them bring much into the house at all. I kept our pantry stocked. Like I had been taught. Enough food to take us through an apocalypse or two.

So it shouldn't have been any surprise when roaches flooded into our kitchen. No amount of sealing off could keep them out of the house. At the hardware store we learned that in Florida—a blend of kudzu and heat, a mixture of North and South, a dangling participle on the United States—they were called palmetto bugs. But they were roaches, all right. We spent the weekends caulking and filling in gaps and trying to figure out how they got in. Roaches don't die easy deaths; they survive nearly everything. A model in which we took solace. Something for us to aspire to.

The Fletchers seemed to turn up just as often. In the middle of our private, shameful behaviors—eating strips of cold steak from the refrigerator, watching sitcoms, tequila-fueled karaoke contests, normal stuff— they rang the doorbell, to ask for something or just to talk.

In the evenings, my husband always tried to say we were on our way out, had just come home, were on the

phone to my frail (and incidentally quite dead) grandmother over the landline to Jamaica. The days were
harder. I wasn't working, and Crystal liked to stop by
to drink my expensive coffee and complain about Ricky.
But mostly she asked questions, each conversation a
kind of song where the response was incredulity. "San
Francisco?" she'd say, as though I'd grown up on the
moon. Or, "Your family's from Jamaica?" before repeat-
ing the tired old stereotypes, the ones about ganja and
the Rastafari. As if my family would ever know Rastafari! Who was she kidding?

Her other favorite topic was our neighbors in the
cul-de-sac, a retired couple and a deaf postal worker.

"They're so fucking stuck-up," Crystal said one day
when she'd cornered me out in the backyard as I pulled
crabgrass from the lawn that was nearly beyond repair.
My husband and I pictured: plastic patio furniture, a
little kettle grill, something Florida, something kitsch.
Watching me at this task, performed in khaki shorts,
would have destroyed my father, whose wedding toast
to my husband had ended with the admonition that if
he was marrying a lady, he better be able to afford the
people that a lady needs in order to be taken care of.

In my mind, it should have been Crystal pulling
that grass while I sat on the porch. "They seem harm-
less," I said.

"Oh, you don't even know the half of it." She sat

with her legs tucked under her on the cracked concrete patio, picking off the ants that migrated to her arms from the nearby anthill.

"What makes you say that?" I asked, throwing another weed into my growing pile.

"Well, like last year when we had a party. That postal bitch called the police, like she could hear anything anyway. And then Ricky got in the cop's face, told him he had a right to have a party any damn time he wanted to."

Even though she didn't continue, I had an idea where that story ended.

"See what I mean?" she said, stretching out her legs. "Total assholes."

At the end of our sixth month in Apopka, the day we saw the RE/MAX sign on the Fletchers' lawn, we celebrated. We went to dinner at an Indian restaurant; we ate tandoori chicken, basket after basket of naan, and my husband touched my leg and looked at me in the same way he had in the back of the taxi. And for the first time ever, we talked about children, imagining who they would be and what they would be like. We chose ridiculous, overly ambitious names: Winston, Phyliss, and Basil. We were optimistic. Here we were, in the only state that offered second chances as readily as orange juice.

We were at last free, even from the Fletchers. The

grass on their lawn turned brown before Ricky backed a U-Haul onto their driveway. From our living room, we pushed aside the drapes and watched as they loaded dressers with missing knobs, an entertainment center that sagged in the middle and was cracked halfway up its side, two badly stained mattresses.

"Should we offer to help them?" my husband murmured next to me as we sprawled on our bellies, peeking at them from the floor. His tone was unenthusiastic.

We watched them try to lift a heavy wood dining table. Watched Ricky drop his end and scream, "Goddamnit, woman, angle it! Just angle it!" Watched Crystal lose her grip on the table. Watched the legs of the table wobble unsteadily on the concrete as Crystal burst into tears.

"I don't think so," I finally said. "They seem to have it under control."

We crawled on hands and knees into the kitchen and made margaritas that we drank out of straws while lying down on the living room floor so they couldn't see our silhouettes moving around in the house. We got so drunk we passed out there and woke up at 4:00 a.m., dehydrated and itchy. We peeked out the window, and their house, usually brightly lit at that hour, was dark, and there was no sign of their car.

It was strange how everything fell apart after they left, as if our mutual hatred of the Fletchers had been holding us together. I caught one cold and then another. A fever sent me to bed for a week and gave me dreams of hazmat suits and children with no noses.

When I came out of it, the squalor of our house was overwhelming. I felt a kind of sadness I couldn't explain. We didn't know it when we'd rented, but our house had been unoccupied for three years. Only we'd been stupid enough to be fooled by a cursory coat of new paint and a neatly trimmed patch of grass. Only we'd been silly enough to walk through the rooms with our landlord, delighting over the built-in mid-century modern table and bookcases, gushing, *This would cost a fortune in San Francisco*. Weren't we delightfully clueless, so much so that we couldn't see the tree rotting in the backyard, that we mistook for rock the artfully placed crystals of desiccants?

Even when I felt better, I lay in bed and spent more days reading magazines in the living room with the air conditioner cranked and went through vodka and orange juice quicker than bread or milk. It was so quiet without the Fletchers. And wasn't it as easy to sink into the sofa as it was into a bottle?

While my husband was at work, I made lists of things to talk to him about when he got home: the fern museum, the Formica that peeled in the second bathroom, the buzzing sounds that sometimes came from the attic during the day. When he got home, I talked at him, until he held up his hands and said, "Enough . . . enough!" And then, "What happened to the living room?"

"The magazines," I said. "I tried to organize the magazines."

They were scattered everywhere, piled on the coffee table and on the chairs.

"I can't come home to this," he said. "Especially if you aren't working." He gave me a funny look. "Are you drinking during the day?" he asked.

And I lied.

Finally, even the bats turned against us. Bats in the belfry, bats in my hair, baby bats starting a new life in our attic. Those bats that we'd watched each evening had taken up residence in our attic. They were up there mocking me, echolocating themselves in colony-wide orgies.

Our empty house with its wide air ducts gave them easy access. They flew through our bedroom. They hung off the ceiling fan. They squeaked and squealed and kept us awake at night, flapping through the yard. One had come up through the bathroom drain and had clearly reported back to his friends. I knew because bat droppings littered the kitchen and one afternoon a wrinkled face peeked from the entertainment center with wide sleepy eyes. And all I could think about were vampires and the scratchy VHS tapes of *Dark Shadows* I'd watched as a kid. My husband chased them with a tennis racket. I was put in charge of finding someone to kill them. The first exterminator said that we couldn't move them, as they'd built a roost filled with tiny bat babies. It violated preservation acts, or at least some kind of natural law. His words, not mine.

The second exterminator told us the baby bats were called pups, as if they were pleasing little dogs instead of leathery clumps. That exterminator's left iris was covered with a thick, milky-white glaze, damaged, I imagined, by the types of chemicals that are used to kill mammalian life, small and large. It was that eye of his that gave me permission to ask how to murder them. Did he have a Shop-Vac? Couldn't he just suck up the pups where they hung—in those gray mucousy-looking sacs?

"I don't think so," he said. "I could lose my license."

"Let's pretend this never happened," I said to him.

Everyone really did get a second chance. Some people got more than that, I told myself over coffee with the third exterminator. He was also a recent transplant to Florida. A recovering meth addict, he was missing most of the hair on his head due to a fire. He'd told his story with a smile, as if remembering a more peaceful time.

My husband offered him money, dinners, companionship, all to entice him into a little bat genocide. The exterminator offered to come back in four months once the bats were old enough to leave the roost on their own.

We talked about abandoning everything, vanishing,

leaving the house to the bats and the roaches, to the mold and the mildew. But our discussions were circular. We kept coming back to my unemployment, our debt. We watched the bats exit the house each night. We drank more wine from plastic cups. We went inside and tried to do a little procreating ourselves. It was animalistic, primal; it was less fun after a week.

We called a fourth exterminator. He was only six months sober, and his hands shook when he lit a cigarette on our patio after inspecting the attic. He stared into the tip as though it was telling him what to say, like it was saving him. When we offered money, he said, "I'm a Christian," and then, "I'm really trying to get my life together."

We ended up keeping our fifty dollars.

"We can't live like this," I said.

"When did exterminators get so ethical?" said my husband.

It was the thick of summer. My long-dead grandmother's trick of hot drinks for cool days was useless when the heat never let up. My husband left the house at 5:00 a.m. to run and came back forty-five minutes later, soaked and panting.

The vegetables I'd planted all that spring shriveled and died. And still at night, there the bats went circling overhead, taunting us. Our landlord's phone was disconnected. Still, we called and hung up, called and hung up. We lived this way for weeks, Fletcher-less, landlord-less, bat infested.

One Saturday we'd had enough and rode our bicycles into town. It was midafternoon. The weather dial on the bank said it was one hundred degrees. We peeled damp shirts from our backs. We ate ice cream and shared bites of mint chocolate chip. Everything felt like it was happening underwater, in slow motion. These other lives. These Florida lives.

"I don't think we're Florida people," my husband said at last. "At least, I'm not."

I didn't respond. This was this thing we did. We were an "us" and then it was "you."

He took another lick of his cone. It was melting fast now, even though we were sitting in the artic chill of the ice cream parlor. The bright green cream ran down his forearm and he chased it with his tongue instead of wiping it with a napkin.

"And what," I said finally, "do you think makes someone a Florida person?"

He shrugged. "I think people who do well here just care less," he said. "To really live here, to really make it home, you have to stop caring."

His face was flat. The opposite of the back of the taxi, the opposite of hiding on the floors from the Fletchers, the opposite of Florida. Maybe he cared too much, but it was the opposite of everything I wanted to be true about him. I wanted to ask him when he thought I stopped caring. When he had started to think about me as different than him. But instead, I took another bite of ice cream.

"Maybe it's the weather," he said finally. "My people aren't built for it. I feel like it must be like this in Jamaica all the time. You have the temperament for it. It's in your DNA. You can stand being uncomfortable."

He was right. I could stand heat. I could stand being uncomfortable. I was from an island of plantation slaves and I knew it. He was from a state of plantation slaves and he had forgotten—or worse, pretended to have forgotten. I wanted him to keep going. To tell me what else I was built for. What else I was good for. Instead, I pretended an accident and knocked the ice cream out of his hand.

He cleaned it up, wiping up the splatters on the table with a napkin. Then chugged water from a bottle he had belted around his waist without offering me a sip.

We were both hot and cranky, I told myself. I was overreacting. We left the ice cream shop and made our way to the library where it was cool, dark, quiet, and heavily air-conditioned. We got library cards. Registered to vote. Felt official. Searched the card catalog for books on bats.

We stayed until the sun started to set, trying to forget that when it did, the roost left our house and went out to collect bugs to bring back for the pups. That was what the books told us. We passed them back and forth on the library tables, pausing every so often to lick the residual stickiness off our fingers and forearms. My husband read about bats that might bite while we slept, infecting us with rabies.

"Where can we get mosquito netting?"

"Where can we get a tarp?"

"Should we sleep in the car?"

"Let's."

We put the bikes in the backyard and crawled into the SUV with provisions. We pushed down the seats, spread out a blanket, opened the sunroof, and poured wine. They came back one or two at a time, and then they blanketed the sky over our heads. We listened to NPR, sipped pinot grigio, and wondered how many nights we could stay like this, smashed into the back seat of our car. We each started to say something, and then stopped. The voices of a call-in talk show about cars washed over us and lulled us to sleep, each on our own side of the SUV.

We called Animal Control in the light of day. We explained the rabies situation. They told us to keep the attic closed, warned us again about the fines.

"We can't stay here," I said. "This isn't working."

There was nowhere else go. We fell back into old habits, doing all those things that we did in the days, weeks, and months before our Florida lives. We bickered until our eyes glazed over before retreating to our separate corners. Sometimes one of us would crack a door. We whispered, *"Are you okay?" "Yes." "No." "Kind of."*

The weight of it all was crushing: money, the past, all the things Florida was supposed to teach us to forget, all the things the silence said were past us. We drank coffee with Baileys, fought, got tired, and fought in other rooms.

I hate you.

I hate you more.

My husband slept on the sofa, and I curled up on the second-bedroom futon. It was like that for weeks. He stopped coming home after work, I stopped cooking dinner, stopped killing palmetto bugs, stopped spraying the back lawn with herbicide and let the crabgrass take over. We became everything we hated, everything we had been in San Francisco. Not all at once, but a little at a time, until we woke up from our separate corners and tried to remember what we loved or even what we liked.

And then they came back, the Fletchers. It had been nearly four months. On a Saturday morning we were grumbling at each other when the pickup truck snaked into the cul-de-sac. I was bleary-eyed at the window, waiting for the coffee to percolate, trying to get in touch with my humanity. They cut the engine before they reached our house, coasted the last few feet and threw up the parking brake. My husband mixed his coffee, not enough cream, too much sugar.

"*It's them!*" I whispered urgently, because I was kind of excited.

"Who?" he asked without turning around.

"Crystal. And Ricky."

They were at our front walk by the time he joined me at the window, and we both stared kind of slack-jawed as they shuffled toward our house. They rang the doorbell, and when my husband threw open the door, we understood why they'd left. Asbestos had been the official reason they'd given us. But standing there on our doorstep, Crystal visibly pregnant, with her T-shirt (*Save the Drama for Your Mama*) barely covering her belly, a sliver of pale, white, taut flesh peeking out—it seemed reason enough.

"Hi!" she squealed, coming in without being invited. She grabbed me in a hard hug. "How've you been?"

Her arms were thin and spindly, but she held me tightly with a warmth I didn't expect.

"Good," I said, trying to squirm out of the embrace. Ricky and my husband shook hands awkwardly and stood around with their hands in their pockets until my husband ushered us all into the living room. He sat on the love seat. I retreated to the couch by the window, wrapping the bathrobe around me.

"We came by to tell you about the baby," she said,

patting her stomach. "My parents bought us one of them new places out near the interstate."

I remembered the advertisements for the new modular homes with imitation granite countertops and laminate flooring that looked like hardwood.

"That's fantastic," my husband said.

"Congratulations," I said.

"And y'all?" Ricky said. "How've y'all been?"

We paused for a moment. I looked at the window with the fucking pink drapes. They clashed with the carpet and the couch and every other thing in the room. "Not good," I said.

I told them about the bats, the attic and the roost, about the damp little pups and the rabies. Tears came to my eyes when I talked about the exterminators.

"Shhhhhhit," Ricky said when I got to the end of my story. "What a mess."

My husband shrugged. "What can you do?" He paused for a moment. "We'll just have to wait it out."

His tone was funny. The same one he'd taken the day with the magazines. The same one he took with me a lot lately, like he couldn't stand me. Like I was an idiot for sharing our misery with these people. These people who weren't friends or family. And maybe he was the one who was uncomfortable, not just in Florida. And maybe I could stand the discomfort, and the Fletchers, and even the bats.

"That bat shit can be dangerous," Ricky said. "I know that much."

I nodded and again felt the tears pricking at the corners of my eyes. I wasn't sure why I was crying. But Ricky was so gentle then. And I started to like him because he was worried about my safety and I thought then that he would be a great father. And I looked at my husband who looked more frightened by my tears than by the warning of the bat shit. And who mouthed, *Stop it.*

"Can I make anyone a drink?" my husband asked, getting up. He didn't wait for an answer, just went into the kitchen where we heard the clatter of ice cubes. Crystal rubbed her belly and Ricky's hands seemed to reach for it too, without even thinking. I imagined how I must have looked to them, standing in a dirty living room, wearing a dirty T-shirt, and framed by several baskets of laundry heaped with clothes both clean and dirty. I'd forgotten which was which. Wasn't I just one set of cartoon bedsheets away from being them?

My husband came back with a pitcher of something red and something sweet and smelling of rum and I knew he was done with the conversation.

"So what you gonna do about them bats, buddy?" Ricky asked, sloshing a drink from the pitcher into a cup.

"Wait it out," my husband said. "Or move."

"Man, that bat shit could make it so y'all can't have kids," Ricky said.

"Let's hope," my husband said, raising his glass, toasting our never babies.

I couldn't look at him then, and so I looked at Crystal, who was shaking her head. "No," she muttered, "no, that's just not right."

Ricky looked at me sternly, like it was a warning, "No, ma'am," Ricky said. "We can't have our friends out here not safe."

And Crystal and Ricky looked at each other, reading each other in a way we never would, never could, no matter how close we tried to be.

There was poison in the back of that truck. Probably enough to render me permanently infertile, definitely enough to give their baby a serious birth defect. But we didn't ask why they had it. The three of us sat amid the crabgrass in the backyard and smoked cigarettes while Ricky went up to the attic with a tea towel tied over his nose and mouth.

Crystal lay in the grass, running though potential baby names. Destiny, Arianna, Duane, Buster. Each sounded more doomed than the last: girls who would end up dancing in clear heels, boys with collections of mug shots instead of school photos. But I asked her for more, and I listened to her explanations of why she liked each and what she hoped for their baby. She wanted a boy. So did Ricky. She wanted a linebacker, a quarterback, but wouldn't be disappointed to get a little girl she could dress real cute.

My husband sat with his back to us, pretended not to listen, and pushed the tips of his fingers together to form a steeple. I wondered if he was thinking the same thing I was. All those talks about those imaginary children we were going to have. Those little pups—young, gifted, and Black—that would be ours.

When Ricky came back it was with three huge, mushy-looking garbage bags filled and tied tightly.

"I just got the babies," he said. "After the others leave tonight, you'll want to seal that attic up nice and tight. Some of them grown ones might die also, but I tried to spray away from them." I felt a little sick listening to him. "Besides," Ricky said, "they won't come back once they find the babies are gone."

Like us, when things didn't work out, they tried to start over somewhere new.

"Thank you," my husband said, shaking his hand.

Crystal and I exchanged another hug.

"You be well," she said, taking my forearms and looking into my face like she was searching. "You call me anytime." She squeezed my arms tightly and said again, "Anytime."

"Take care," I said. "It was good to see you. I'll see you real soon."

And I got it then, that they were mine—Crystal and Ricky. They understood something about Florida life that my husband never would. They understood starting over, and sadness, and frustration. They understood what it meant when you needed a second chance or a third or a fourth. They understood something about us or about me that my husband didn't—wouldn't. Maybe my husband had seen that. I was a Florida person after all.

That night we dragged the chairs out for the last time. The evening sun had just begun to dip in the sky, and the houses in the cul-de-sac were lit with a deep orange glow, making them look less like prefabricated shacks and more like cottages, places where anyone could be happy.

We knew then that we were done. Done with our Florida lives, done with each other. Tomorrow, or the day after, one of us would leave. We would split the contents of the ramshackle house and try to start over again, without drinking, without each other.

The two of us were quiet for a moment, looking all around us instead of at each other, until finally my husband opened the bottle of chardonnay, slick with sweat, and poured the yellow wine into plastic cups. We knocked them slightly and toasted the Fletchers, the palmetto bugs, the bats. We toasted new beginnings, real and imagined, the cool crisp air of the San Francisco Bay, the smoky heat of an Apopka afternoon, and this night, too, heavy with the weight of the future. We watched the first one or two bats come out from the top of the house. Lights turned on, and a blue-green glow began to come from the other homes in the cul-de-sac, each window lit up like a beacon as the sky got darker and darker.

And then, all of a sudden, out flew the bats, a thick black sheet, flying so close to our heads we could almost touch them and we heard the meaty thumps of their wings. They moved out and up, away from the house, away from their dead babies. The last part of our Florida lives, gone into the last bit of purple wilting in the sky before it went completely black.

Shopgirl

You WILL SPEND your entire life selling—but this is the first time. So small, you barely reach the counter. You are given a stool. You are told if you work hard, there will be a reward. You are taught to make change. You are taught to make smiles at the customers. You are taught to cut yam, to chop pigs' feet, to take hot patties from the hotter oven. The burns and scrapes and cuts will last through adulthood, will last beyond death. Injury will always remind you of what it means to work.

On Saturday morning, the shop is clotted with people from the Islands, all there to buy oxtail, and pigs' feet, to take packages of tripe, leaking, wrapped in heavy butcher paper—and to argue and laugh, and laugh and argue. They lean toward bags of Otaheite apples, or cho-cho, or tins of *Milo*. If only you could inhale the coming future in which these foods will become fashionable, in which this education in butchery, in food and flavor, will twenty and more years later help you appear hip and cultured—exotic, even—to lighter-skinned friends in particular. You can't now know, but you will be the lonely one who understands how blood thickens stew, how marrow complicates flavor, how the perfect pepper in the bin needs to be found.

Forget this work? No. Never. This work defines you, contains you. Allows you. But much later, your friends somehow think you spent your early years traveling— not, in fact, in the back room of a small shop inside a strip mall, listening to the high musical Bajans remind you that *Coward dog keep whole bone.* Listening to the Trinis insist, *Better belly buss than good food waste.* And the Jamaicans, the Jamaicans, measuring out mutton with their eyes, asking, *Just a toops more fi make mi belly na cry fi hunga.* Floors always need sweeping, candies kept clean, not to eat. You dust shelves stocked with things you cannot imagine your white friends at school eating: guava jelly, tamarind paste, cock soup. At the shop there's always, always a cricket match on the small portable television, and everyone complaining about the gassed bananas and eating gizzada and bun and pro-cessed cheese that comes in a tin. How can you explain this, any of it? Your history with food, with work, the way they are fastened together? The way that you love and hate the shop equally?

Your parents don't understand the shame of Monday morning. Don't know what it means to have fish scales on your pink Keds, or what it means that your hair smells like brown stew chicken, or that your sandwich is corned beef and salad cream between two thick slices of hard dough bread, or that a boy tells you it looks like mashed brains so you look down and chew and chew and chew. You won't know for years that it tasted like home and that gift of the British to both plant a flag and impose a culture.

On Saturday you will hear—over and over again—*It's so good to have the whole family here. Working.* Over and over again—all day—you will hear it, thinking of other girls your age in ballet classes. Sleeping in. Shopping with their mothers. Settling into Saturday-morning cartoons. And bowls of Cap'n Crunch. You sweep floors, cut dasheen, and try to read when you can, waiting for the book to be snatched from your hands. *This shop is your story, your inheritance.* Over and over again—as you haul ten-pound bags of basmati, stack tins of coconut milk. *I'm glad you are doing it. Just like the Chinese. We need to be more like them.* You will remember *Oliver Twist* (which you read in snatches between tasks) and the workhouse and Fagin. And you can't imagine why someone won't come and save you, too. But you remember that these are your real parents, that these Saturdays are your real life. That this world of shop chat, bleaching cream, boxes of dasheen, copies of *The Gleaner* with newsprint so smeared that you can barely read the stories, and cartons of goat milk and everything beyond it is yours and also not yours. You will always associate work with the coppery smell of animal blood and sawdust and blades that cut fish.

If you could, you'd squint and look into the future. Tell the customers—so much in love with your work, with your working—that the Chinese and everyone but them will own their Island one day. Hurt them. If you could, you would look down, fold your arms, suck your teeth, and tell them that you won't remember them fondly. You can't know if they will remember you with fondness either—or perhaps at all. You—the little girl, swinging with effortless precision, wielding that machete—the magic of it all. You close your eyes and the rest of you becomes the machete, too. Cutting through their dreams, as they lie in bed, their bellies full. Will they remember the sound of the blade cutting meat, cutting bone, before it thuds home on the butcher's block? Will they remember who did the selling? Or will they only remember buying?

You will just remember the work.

Weaving

DELROY HAS ONLY thirty more minutes before the fight. He is sitting in one of the warm-up rooms off the gym's main ring. It's one of six other rooms where he imagines all the other fighters are getting ready, too. Just a piece of dingy gray curtain separates him from the scrape of the chairs as people sit down, get comfortable, wait for the show. They usually start with the feather-weights. Tonight, he fights second.

People are a lot easier, more fun to hit than punching bags. People duck and weave and bob, and they throw punches, but they also let you strategize, and that's what gets Delroy excited. When he moves his body around a person and knows what they are going to do, it makes him feel powerful, invincible, it's almost as good as be-ing high.

Just now, though, he can feel the heft of tonight's

fight. He warms up on the bag and hits it as hard as he can as it sways back and forth, taunting him. *Such a loser, Delroy. You ain't never gonna be a good fighter, Delroy. Dellllllroy, Delllllroy! Hit me harder, Delroy! You won't hurt me none with those little sissy punches, old man.*

The bag is a mean motherfucker and Delroy hits it harder and harder until his lungs feel empty and sweat runs down his forehead and stings his eyes. He is happy to have that bag to warm up on, and when he is good and warm, he hugs it, worrying how he is going to look at Fanakov and put up any kind of a fight.

He bounces back and forth on the balls of his feet, trying to stay loose and limber. Fanakov is pretty young—can't be more than nineteen or twenty—and he has a mean look. When they weighed in, Fanakov had looked him up and down and laughed before coming over to introduce himself. Delroy had tried to pretend that he cared, like he really wanted to take the little prick. "Have respect, son," he'd muttered under his breath and even added a few extra looks for good measure. Truth is, it's Sunday now and he doesn't really care. It's all a show. It's just a show. He's going to get his ass handed to him and when that's done, he'll visit the dumpster behind the gym. Then he'll clean himself off in that bathroom with the mud-colored water. And then he'll go home and drink until he gets the spins and passes out. There aren't reasons to fight anymore.

He doesn't remember what the reasons were in the first place.

Two days ago when he'd called, he asked his ex-wife what the kid wanted for her birthday and she snorted into the phone. "What can you afford to get her?"

He wanted to tell her he'd give anything, every-thing, but the woman was right; he couldn't even pay the court-ordered child support. He wanted to tell her that things could change for him after this fight, but she had heard it all before and then her voice got that hard edge to it, the kind that could floor him as easily as an uppercut to the jaw. They'd been divorced seven years now and she had a new husband—a rich white guy who'd bought a big house with a swimming pool. And it wasn't that he hated the man. What he hated was the way his ex-wife made him feel like he'd been a detour, an experiment, something she tried on and returned be-fore she started her real life.

On the day they were married at city hall, even her eyes had been smiling, looking at him like he was the future. That day, she'd teased her blond hair so big that it looked like candy floss and she'd worn a pink dress and pink eye shadow and penciled in a mole above her lip. She'd been so beautiful. It was just the two of them. Her parents were what she'd called old Philadelphia

Mainliners. He didn't know what it meant then and he still didn't. Whatever the meaning, he understood that they hadn't approved of her marrying a Black man. But she had never looked more happy in her life. And, at the time, it was his happiest day, too.

Now, she hadn't invited him to his daughter's birthday. She mentioned that there was a party, but she didn't say anything about him coming. So, he was going. Fuck her. She wasn't keeping him away from the kid.

He got on the road right after his workout. He left later than he planned, later than he should've, and then he had to borrow the money for gas. He owed so much money at this point he didn't have any shame about borrowing a little more. What difference was another fifty dollars going to make?

In the car he turned on the radio. Never any reggae here, but the Motown songs reminded him of growing up in Trench Town. There had been some American music in Jamaica then, and he remembered the way the American girls on the radio would sing *sha la-la* at the end of a verse. He didn't remember the names of those groups, not like he remembered Millie Small or songs by the Skatalites.

Even though it was nearly twenty-five years ago, what he remembered was the *sh, sh sh* sounds of a brush against those drums—hard and soft all at once, like the girls that he would press up to in the back rooms of those dance halls when he first moved to Kingston. He was a country boy and he'd never seen girls like that. Girls in linen dresses, their eyes lined with thick, black makeup that made them look like cats. Those girls who always looked so soft, but when he tried to catch their eye, they turned bored and hard. Sometimes, he'd manage a dance and rest a hand lightly on a shoulder or hip. He looked down and tried to move his hips like he'd seen his uncles and his brothers do. Those late-night rocksteadies were nothing like the parties he went to when he got to America, even when the music sounded the same. He turned the volume up in the truck and sang along to the American music that was still foreign and also familiar.

> Now if I appear to be carefree
> It's only to camouflage my sadness . . .

The town where his ex-wife lived was as far on the outskirts of Philadelphia as you could get. You had to pass the Amish and all that other shit before you got to Millersville. He felt the space of each blink getting longer and longer and he turned on his high beams, lighting up the road so that he could push through the darkness inside and outside of the truck. He scratched the back of his head, imagining the dandruff scattering on the sleeve of his jacket, like it was snowing inside the truck, too.

He'd seen a picture of a little kid–sized carousel in a magazine four years ago, around the time of his daughter's birthday when he was waiting in a clinic for a doctor to patch up a gash in his head after a fight. It had a white horse and a lion. He'd pictured his baby girl riding around in a ruffled dress and imagined the way she would scream, partly in terror and partly in joy, the smile on her face big and bright. And so he'd torn the picture out of the magazine. But when he called to ask for the price, some man told him it cost three thousand dollars. He couldn't even imagine what that kind of money would look like gathered all in one place.

But this year—what was it, her tenth?—he was going to get her something even better. Something that she could keep much longer than a blasted carousel. A pig. A baby pig for his baby girl. Every little girl loved animals. Something to snuggle with. And baby piglets were small, easy to cuddle, better than any goddamn stuffed animal. 'Cause it was real. And 'cause he knew all about pigs—how they looked, what they tasted like, what you fed them—and he could help her.

His daddy had raised pigs and Delroy smelled the pig shit on every letter that came to him from Trelawny Parish. The words were always written in pencil with a light hand, and with spellings that he could barely understand until he stopped trying to understand at all. He didn't want to remember that home in Cockpit

Country, that time before he'd gone to Kingston and seen himself for what he was—a rusty-headed pickney who smelled like animals and who didn't understand a damn thing about the world. His father hardly made enough to feed Delroy and his two younger sisters, so he sent off Delroy first to live with an older brother in Kingston and then to an auntie in Philadelphia at age eighteen.

Twice he'd scraped together the money to bring his mother and father to America, but the visits were short and mostly his parents watched him out of the corners of their eyes, not sure what to say about him, about his blond wife, or about the way he pummeled men.

"Lord have mercy, what you expect to come to, beating men?" his father had asked him after watching Delroy work out during one of the visits. "What you need to learn is a skill, a trade, something that will carry you along the road of life."

But Delroy couldn't tell his father, or anyone else, that he felt he was his smartest, his best self when his fist connected solidly to someone's jaw, or when he made another man double over in pain. So Delroy just looked down and nodded.

There was a farm he remembered from the last time he'd driven out there six years ago. It was only about twenty miles outside of the town where his ex-wife lived, and it was a small farm, probably only a farmer and his wife. He worried that it would now be gone, but as he came over the hill, he could make out the silhouette of the farmhouse even though it had grown dark. These country stars and that big moon lit the sky well enough for him to see the house and, behind it, the large barn and, farther back still, the pen and stalls.

Even in the dark he could tell where they kept the pigs. He knew the smell just as well as he knew the smell of himself—the sour corncobs, rotting potato peels, and grain mixed with apples, which his father said made the animal's flesh sweeter. He climbed the fence slowly and lowered himself into the pigpen. Luck was with him, the sow looked ready to pop, but then Delroy saw that she'd already had her babies. She lay on her side, her eyes closed, piglets suckling at her teats. She groaned, a sound that came from deep inside her, but she didn't move. There were no male pigs in the pen, only the mother and her piglets. He wondered if a boar laid claim to family, if he tried to protect them. He wondered if this crime was worse than stealing, ripping apart a family, taking a baby from its mother. The thought shadowed his mind for a while, and he swallowed hard, trying to let it go.

The sow opened one eye, but she seemed uninterested. Maybe she had an idea that she and her piglets would end up someone's breakfast or wallet and she could not muster interest. Whatever it was, he was glad.

He had seen sows get angry, rush a man, make people sorry. You had to be ready for situations like that, so he got in his stance, crouched low, and braced himself. He stopped breathing for a moment or two, knees bent, ready to jump the low fence again if the sow chose to attack. But the sow didn't stir—she just lay on her side, eyes shut, while being manhandled by those greedy piglets. He walked up slowly and moved behind her head, stroking it gently. She leaned gratefully into the caress like a dog, her eyes still shut.

The piglets reminded him of what his daughter looked like when she was first born, all wriggly, small, and hairless. Delroy was in the hospital that day, but even then, he'd known that he and the wife were already done. He never hit her. Never. He knew some fighters who hit their wives, who beat them as bad as they beat any man in the ring. But not him.

His wife glared at him the entire time she was giving birth, like he was the one hurting her. He sat in the corner, watching, and when it was all over, she held the little bundle that would have her father's dark skin and her mother's blue eyes. He stayed in the corner and stared—feeling dumb—and wondering how he was going to make the kid love him. When they finally let him hold her, he knew he had to do anything for her. No. He had to do everything for her.

There weren't many times to fall in love. It had

happened only three times, and each had seemed to come out of nowhere. The first was a grocery store clerk, the second, his ex-wife, and the third was his baby girl. But just like everything, he messed it up. He swore he would try to do better with this little girl. He thought it would be kind of like fighting; when you loved, you could anticipate the hurt just like you could anticipate the punch. Treating people like shit was his best strategy to avoid direct blows. He would do better with her. That day in the hospital, he'd promised himself.

Years later, drinking in some dive bar or getting his eye stitched up after a fight, he thought about that pig. "That pig," he said. "That goddamn pig was the only one I did right for love."

It would be a lie. He didn't know how to do anyone right, not for love or anything else. But he liked the way the story sounded, the way that it tacked neatly against the idea of who he was instead of the reality. Later on in its retellings, he became more magical, and he spun a story about his little girl and the piglet and how their bellies would get fat together. His little girl would love the pig, and she would always remember the daddy who brought it for her. When you raised something, you could take some pride in it. He didn't raise his daughter and so he could only be proud in a faraway kind of way, feeling some ownership while knowing at the same time he had nothing to do with the success.

•

He lifted the sow's back leg and discovered a piglet fast asleep with a full belly. As a boy, they'd only ever picked up the piglets on his father's farm to castrate them. The smell of their sex tainted the meat, made it taste thick with the kind of desire that he didn't understand until he was grown. The male piglets who weren't fixed were mean as hell, and before he was his daughter's age, he'd learned to stay away. He gently lifted the tiny creature out from under its mother and immediately it began to shiver. It made little half grunts, half squeals in its sleep and Delroy made sure it was a girl before tucking the piglet inside his down jacket. He felt the piglet move instinctually to his heat or to his heart. He smiled in the dark, dank pen, feeling the piglet's body warm against his own.

He ran out to his truck before the thing could realize it was being stolen. Back in the cab of his truck, he sang to the piglet like he wanted to sing to his baby girl. He knew all those old Jackson Five songs, and he could sing a falsetto like Michael if he tried real hard, but his voice was naturally rough and low, and eventually he stopped singing and started coughing. A rib had healed badly the last time his opponent had broken one. When he leaned over, he could feel a sharp stab radiating outward on his left side, his intercostal muscles no longer firm and tight. The piglet vibrated against his chest with each dry, hacking breath he took. It squealed and he pulled the animal tightly against him.

"Don't cry," he murmured. "Everything will be all right."

The pig whined, and then its pitch got higher and louder. It squealed louder than he could have ever imagined.

"Damnit!" he yelled out over the screaming piglet.

Finally, he saw his ex-wife's house, so he pulled the truck over on the shoulder and unzipped the jacket where the tiny thing had shit itself as it continued to screech and wriggle against him. He roughly tossed the animal away from him, down onto the passenger-side floorboard, on top of an old pair of boxing gloves. Delroy wiped at the shit with a napkin he found tucked into the seat. The piglet ran around and squealed even louder. He mashed his hands over his ears.

"Stop it!" he shouted.

But the animal was frightened. It ran underneath the truck's wider seat and Delroy could hear it under there, crying and breathing hard. He sat back for a second and closed his eyes. Not only was he late, but now he was late and smelled like pig shit.

There was one light on outside, but the rest of the house looked dark. Someone had strung pink crepe paper up over the porch. The clock on the truck's radio flashed 2:00 over and over. The piglet was crying softly, a small mewling sound, almost like a kitten, and he couldn't stand it. He decided to leave it in the truck. Holding the thing, he realized, might end up causing more problems. The porch stairs creaked as he put his weight on them. Delroy rang the doorbell three times in a row. There was movement in the house. A light in the upstairs window. He pounded on the glass in the door hard enough to make his hand hurt.

"I'm coming," he heard from inside. "Stop the pounding! I'm coming!"

"Delroy?" she said, opening the door just a crack. "It's almost eleven. What are you doing here?"

"I came for the party," he said.

"Are you insane?" That was the way his ex spoke to him, like he was an idiot. He remembered how much he hated her. The last time he had seen her, she threw things at him. A shoe and a bottle of nail polish, the two things she could get her hands on the quickest. He'd brought the little girl back late. She had called him a kidnapper.

Her hair was tied back in a scarf and she had on a pink bathrobe. She was still skinny but her face looked old. She scowled at him, her body outlined in the doorframe, everything else behind her dark.

"I brought Jenny a gift."

She was silent for a second, and then, "A gift? Her

party ended hours ago, and you show up here at, what? Almost midnight? What the hell do you think this is? A nightclub?" Her voice went up on the last word and she shook her head.

"I got here as quickly as I could." He looked down. "Is she awake?"

She laughed the hard laugh he hated so much. It made him want to grab her by the bathrobe, to pull her close enough that she'd feel his anger, to drape her up and drag her in close to his fist, to make her feel what it meant to be disrespected. He wanted her to understand how badly he wanted to hit her, but that he didn't, that he wouldn't.

"No, she isn't awake. She went to bed three hours ago, and I'm not waking her." Her voice got louder.

"Damnit." He shifted his weight from foot to foot. He could feel himself getting angry. "Come on, I drove all the way out here and I got a present for her in the truck."

Another light flicked on and he looked past her, into the house and down the hall. The husband was there. He was backlit and Delroy couldn't see his face. But he wasn't afraid of that punk. He could take him. He'd taken men twice his size.

"Is there a problem?" the husband asked as he came up behind her.

"No, baby," she said, turning toward him. She

touched the man's face in a way that he couldn't ever remember her touching his. "I can handle him," she said to her husband. "Go back to bed. Please."

But the man stayed. She turned back toward Delroy.

"This asshole thinks I'm going wake Jenny at midnight."

"You *are* gonna wake her," Delroy insisted, raising his voice. "You ain't gonna keep my child away from me."

"Oh really, Delroy," she said. "You got some loser friends to come help you out? Oh, or maybe you could get the police and tell them how you never pay your child support? Yeah, maybe then."

Her husband seemed to shrink behind her then, and he muttered something that Delroy couldn't hear as she started to push the door shut. Who did she think she was? Who did they think they were? They didn't own his daughter. He had just as much right to the girl as they did. He smashed his fist against the door, causing it to kick back into her shoulder and arm. It surprised her, scared her, maybe, and she stumbled backward.

"You better let me in," Delroy said, his voice low. "I don't think that you wanna mess with me tonight."

His knuckle had split and he'd smeared blood against the pretty white paint on the French-style doors. He could feel the blood rushing through his veins, down his arms, and into his fists. She wasn't going to make him into a joke tonight. She wasn't going to go back into that house and have a good laugh at his expense with that fancy husband. He pushed harder against the door. He wanted to cry and he wanted to scream at the same time. He wanted to smash the whole door to pieces. He wanted to smash the world to pieces.

"Don't you touch me, Delroy," she screamed. "I'll make you sorry."

She'd already made him sorry. No, tonight she was going to be the one who was sorry, the one who felt guilty and angry and sorry. She pushed the door back harder and he pushed, too. Then it fell open and he almost stumbled into the house. The husband had jerked the door open.

"Delroy, I think you'd better go."

The husband's face was smooth as a college kid's, and his haircut looked expensive. There was something about him that looked delicate, almost like a woman. His skin was pale, almost translucent, a network of veins right below the surface. Delroy was close enough that he could see that his eyelashes were wispy and blond, and his brows were nearly invisible, and they scared Delroy for a second. But he knew there was no way this man had his strength, his stamina, or his hook. The man steadied himself and gently pushed Delroy's ex-wife back into the house. But Delroy could see that she wanted a fight. She stood behind her husband, pointing and yelling. Trying to make Delroy mad. This was how he usually remembered her. This was how she'd always been, always trying to pick a fight, getting him riled up until he broke something or hit something or slammed a door. Toward the end of things between them, it got to be so that he started to think she liked to see him that way, that she got off on seeing him lose his mind.

"No," Delroy said. "I don't think I better had. I think you had better let me see my daughter for her birthday."

"You're six hours late," the husband said. "We have rules in this household, and we expect everyone to abide by them. You included, Delroy."

Delroy hated him. He looked out toward his truck. He thought about that baby pig in there. He thought about how little he'd seen of his daughter's growing-up time. All he wanted to do was to give her the present. He would barely recognize her now; she was nine, no, ten years old now, almost a woman. This was the last good time to give her a piglet.

"You're a mess," the husband said. "And you smell. Is this really how you want to see your daughter? How you want her to see you?"

The husband took a step back into his house—that big house with its porch and all those windows, that house he was rich enough to afford. Let him get his own daughter. The husband started to shut the door.

"Go sleep and take a shower for Chrissake before

coming back to see your child. And calling first wouldn't hurt."

When he first stated boxing he came to every match like it was a street fight, like it was one of the brawls he'd had on the streets of Trench Town, hitting as hard as he could, landing blows wherever he could, below the belt, in the kidneys, headbutting and wrestling. He'd lost so many times like that, lost even though he should have won. And still he kept on being disqualified until he got a trainer and learned the rules. Even then, he would forget and hit on a break after the bell or forget to go back to his corner after he'd knocked a fighter down. The rules had never been his strong suit, lost him money more times than he could count. But what was he supposed to do here?

He'd gotten up lots of times, his face pulpy, his spirit in a worse condition. He might not win but he wasn't done until everything was beat out of him. Delroy took a step forward. He caught the doorjamb with the back of his hand.

"No, man, I don't think I'll be doing that tonight," Delroy said. "I think I'll just be seeing my daughter, thank you very much."

Delroy took a step into the house, and just like in the ring, he could sense when the first punch was coming. The husband swung at him like a man who'd never been in a fight. His fist landed on Delroy's forehead. It wasn't much, but it did hurt. Delroy took his stance, tucked his chin, and jabbed the guy in the nose. He hit hard enough to draw blood.

She screamed. When you hit someone in the nose, the blood almost always spurted. It was like he'd turned a faucet. Blood went down the front of the husband's expensive T-shirt, all over the nice expensive carpet and the bathrobe his ex-wife was wearing. Delroy hoped he'd broken the son of a bitch's nose. He hoped that it ended up crooked; he hoped he'd destroyed his pretty face.

"Delroy!" she shrieked. "You stupid fuck!"

He felt her comment all the way down to his toes, because it always came back to his intelligence with her. He was an idiot to laugh at, and he imagined her shaking her head and remembering when she was stupid enough to love him.

She shoved and beat at Delroy before she saw about her husband. His hands were cupped around his nose. He looked up for a second, and Delroy saw that he was thinking about trying to hit him again.

"I just want to see my kid," Delroy said.

"It's always about hitting with you, isn't it, Delroy? You don't have an ounce of class and you never will," his ex-wife screeched at him. "Are you all right, baby?

Are you okay?" she asked, turning to her husband. She tried to move his hands from his nose, but the blood was everywhere.

"Don't touch me," he said.

Neither of them could bother with the door anymore. The husband walked away down the hall. He left blood on the carpet and she followed him. For a moment, it was as if they'd forgotten about Delroy.

He thought for a second about the pig in the truck. He decided that it would be fine. Pigs were resilient animals.

The little girl was sleeping when he went into her room. Kids that age could sleep through a hurricane, Delroy thought. She didn't look anything like he remembered. He watched her chest move up and down for a while before he shook her shoulder.

"Wake up, Jenny," he said roughly because he didn't know any other way to say it.

"What?" she murmured. She sat up in bed, her hair messy and sticking out at odd angles.

"Who are you?" she asked, rubbing her eyes.

She said it with no kind of fear. Just some strange man sitting in her bedroom, and she was casual about it. It hurt him worse than his hand, which was starting to bleed again.

"I'm your daddy."

"No," she said flatly. "You're not."

"Yes," he said. "I am."

She stared at him as best she could in her bedroom, half-lit by the light in the hall. Peered at him with a look he recognized from her mother's face, suspicious and searching.

"No," she decided. "You're not."

She lay back down in her little bed and turned away from him.

She was even better at jabs than her mother. But he got back up again, went back into the ring.

"Jenny," he said, shaking her shoulder again. "Wake up."

She rolled over and sat up again.

"What?" she asked, exasperated. He was surprised at her annoyance. He wanted to get mad, but he couldn't.

"I'm your daddy and I came for your birthday. Remember I saw you when you turned four and we went to the zoo and got ice cream?"

Her eyes narrowed. She thought hard.

"Yes," she said finally. "But your face looked different then."

"Well, I'm a fighter and I get banged up pretty bad." He pointed to the deep scar above his right eye and the angry welt raising on his forehead.

She stared at him a moment and shrugged.

"I remember you got ice cream on my dress," she said accusingly.

He laughed. She had fussed at the dress, blotting at it with napkins and insisting over and over that chocolate stained.

"Well, my party was this afternoon," she said. "You're late now and I'm tired."

She lay back down again and turned away from him.

"I brought you something, baby," he said to her back, not wanting to see the blue eyes flash at him again.

"What is it?" she said, not turning toward him. "I got everything I wanted."

"I got you a pet."

He had her attention now and she flipped over to face him.

"A puppy?" she said excitedly.

"No. Better."

She laughed. That same hard laugh as her mother. "There's nothing better than a puppy."

"It's a piglet, honey, your very own to play with and cuddle."

She made a face.

He furrowed his brow. "Nothing could love you more than a little pig."

"No one has a pig," she said, exasperated. "They're gross."

He felt the slap of her words across his heart. He got up from the bed and went over to the window. There was a thing in her face, a smile at the corners of her mouth that made him see that she wanted to do this. She wanted to make him feel like a piece of shit. And she had. He came away from the window, into the shadow so she couldn't see his eyes. He wouldn't cry. He wouldn't give her the satisfaction. Instead he twisted his face into a grimace, he squared his hips and punched the air a few times. He bounced around on the balls of his feet and flexed his left biceps. He wanted to show her what it looked like in the ring when he was winning, even though he was losing so badly right now. *Look at me*, he wanted to say, *I'm something. I'm really something.* She peered at him from the bed and rolled her eyes. She knew. She knew she had flattened him. She sat up and took her stance, ready to knock him out.

"You can keep it," she said. "I don't want it."

"No," he said, standing over her. "No, damnit, I came out here to bring you a pig and you're gonna take that pig."

She opened her eyes widely.

"No," she said. "Don't you understand. *N-O*." There was something in her tone that reminded him again of his ex-wife and he pulled away from her.

"Yes," he hollered. "You're taking it."

The husband was at the door.

"Are you all right, Jenny?" he asked.

"Yeah, Dad, I'm fine. He"—she said, gesturing toward Delroy—"wants to force me to take a pig."

She glared at Delroy, her eyes narrowed.

"Don't worry," the husband said to her. "Just go back to bed; I'll take care of everything."

Delroy knew then that he wouldn't see his daughter again. He followed the husband out of the little girl's bedroom and into the hallway. The husband closed the door behind Delroy as he left the room.

"You better leave," the husband said to him. "The police are on their way."

He was holding a giant wad of tissue to his nose. He shoved Delroy a little as he hustled him out of the house. Delroy took it.

When he opened the truck door the pig was dead. The strings from his boxing gloves were wrapped around its neck. He held it in his hands and felt for a heartbeat. Its tongue was hanging out of its little mouth. He stroked the pig's belly and wrapped it up in some old newspapers that were in the back of his truck. When he was done, he laid the animal on the seat. He climbed out of the truck and vomited on his ex-wife's front yard. The vomit splattered up on his shoes and pants.

He drove all through the night. He'd thought about not returning at all. He'd thought about just turning the truck west and driving out to Las Vegas and ruining himself in whatever way he could. But something made him turn around. Hell, it wasn't some unknown thing. It was money. He'd spent the last of it on gas and a joint.

Tonight it is just Fanakov and him. The first fight is ending. In the locker room, Deloy can hear the muted cheers of the crowd. They sound so far away. He is next. He jumps rope for a minute, and then makes sure his bucket has Vaseline, extra rags, and a first-aid kit. This place—with its metallic smell, a combination of sweat and piss, the rusted lockers, the torn shreds that pass for a curtain and the animals out there, the ones that want to watch him beat the other guy to the brink of death. This is as far as he was ever going to get. The fluorescents flicker and he breathes deeply. He isn't ever going to be the main event. He might be a tomato can after this fight. A fighter not good enough to be a champion but one who was smart enough and experienced enough for the better fighters to spar with without getting hurt.

The newspaper-wrapped pig is stiff and shoved in the back of his locker inside his duffel. He has priors and couldn't risk leaving it in the truck. It isn't like he wants to keep it, and he doesn't know why he hasn't dumped the thing already. He can't figure why he has held on to the thing for two days and a night. But for some reason it feels hard to let the animal go. In his kitchen he'd wrapped it in an old towel and in news-paper and in plastic wrap and a zip-top baggie to keep it from smelling. The baggie is in the locker, tucked alongside his street clothes and extra tape, and in spite of his work, when he opens the locker door, the sickly smell of death—the one he is getting used to—creeps up through the old sweat and blood of the locker room. Later tonight, after the fight, he will pitch it in the dumpster with the empty beer cups and the swept-up peanuts. He needs to be done with it, even if he isn't sure that he wants to be.

The call bell rings. His fight is only five minutes away. He picks up the joint next to the plastic bag. His sweat wets the paper but the weed still crackles when he lights it. He holds the smoke in his lungs as long as he can and then coughs it out. He massages his lower back where the muscles are tight.

He doesn't hardly like smoking this shit anymore. But he needs to feel loose, to feel light on his feet. But it takes a lot to get the same feeling he had at twenty. He inhales again, hard, and holds the smoke in his lungs. The weed isn't very good. He barely feels anything, but he finishes it because he doesn't want to waste it. He would like to school Fanakov. To show him that he's been in the game longer, that he can tell him what's what. But taking the beating is what he is planning to do. He will get at least seventy-five dollars for the ass whipping. Not much, but enough. Enough to get by. The prize for the winner is five hundred dollars.

And then he is in the ring. And the announcer says both their names and all he can think about is the fact that Fanakov's name sounds like he might be Russian, just like the name of his wife's new husband might be. Like the last name they might force on his daughter, and he gets pissed off. He starts pummeling the kid, but Fanakov fights back, works his midsection mostly. And as he hits the kid in the face, he remembers that other man's face covered in blood. And then he has the kid on the ropes and he is hitting him as hard as he can. He forgets all about his daughter, her birthday party, his ex-wife's new husband. He just thinks about how good it feels punching the kid. He thinks that maybe he could win this thing. Leave the place tonight with five hundred dollars in his pocket.

But Fanakov is fast and young. He hits Delroy with a looping crosspunch that he doesn't see coming and he is pushed back against the ropes, but only for a second. He thinks about what he has to do tonight after the fight. And all the nights that will come after that, and he is steady on his feet again.

He gives the kid a swift uppercut, knocking him on his ass for a second. The kid looks up at him and Delroy doesn't know what the kid sees in his face. Whatever it is makes him scramble to his feet quickly. And then they are both punching as hard as they can, punches coming until Delroy has no idea who is winning and who is losing and he doesn't want to, because he's wondering how many chances he has left to beat a man.

All-Inclusive

ANAYA MET THE Poet seven years earlier during Carnival in Trinidad. Her modeling agency had hired her out to a rum company. Her job for the week was to be beautiful, to smile, and to hand out drinks to dignitaries and specially invited guests. The Poet was there at the behest of the Trinidadian president. He was from Jamaica, Anaya from LA. But her whole family was from Jamaica, her parents and grandparents and their grandparents, all those generations who had cut cane and picked cacao and fought the British. In her hot-pink bikini covered with crystals, a cerulean Carnival headdress with rhinestones and feathers dripping down her back—she imagined that she looked like the waves of the Island that tied them together.

Later, at a cocktail party at the president's house in Port of Spain, overlooking the botanical gardens on a balcony, the Poet pressed a drink into her hand, pulling her so close she felt the bristles on his chin against her cheek, the heat of the rum on his breath as he whispered into her ear, *"My eyes grew dim, and I could no more gaze; / A wave of longing through my body swept."* It was a line like any other, not particularly clever. But at the time she'd thought it was original, thought he'd composed the words just for her and it made her feel special. It wasn't until years later that she realized that the Poet hadn't written it, that his tribute to the beauty of Jamaican women had been borrowed from Jamaican poet Claude McKay's "The Tropics in New York." A line from a poem as old as him. And she'd fallen for it.

How could she have been reeled in? Wasn't everything in her DNA recoiling from him and his estate in Port Antonio, his pale skin ruddied by too much sun, nearly matching the pale pink guayabera he wore? Somehow—the poem? the flattery? his age? his money? It was all of it and it worked, like she imagined it always had for him. And then they were together.

He needed her, he said. He couldn't write, he said. He couldn't breathe, couldn't eat without her. Sometimes, if she railed enough, sometimes he would tell her he was going to leave his wife. Sometimes, if she wasn't disciplined enough, she thought there might be another woman. Not his wife, of course, but another woman like *her*—dark-skinned, dark-bodied, a child of conquest, a

woman to keep. Because if he kept her, couldn't he collect another one like her just as easily?

At home in California, she found herself googling
him, looking at all of the pictures of him, straining to
find evidence. She enlarged the images, checking to
see if he had a hand on another woman's shoulder or
around her waist. This was how she spent her breaks
during her shitty jobs: Scrolling crouched in a toilet at a
West Hollywood club where she sold shots on weekend
nights. Scrolling in her parked car and smoking a cigarette during the lunch shift at the Covina Steakhouse
where she waited tables. Scrolling while she waited
for her name to be called on audition after audition
for parts that she wasn't going to get. This was how it
was . . . picture after picture on a Google Images search
of him in a crisp black tux. If there were pictures of
her on the Internet, they would be of her scraping dried
mashed potatoes off her waitress pants. She never dated
anyone else; she just complained about how superficial
dating was in LA when people asked her if she was seeing someone.

Soon the trips began. They met in Madrid. And
New York. They sat on beaches, they hiked in caves,
they helicoptered over volcanoes. When she and Poet
were together, she was convinced that she had been
silly to doubt him, that there was no possible way he
wanted anyone but her. He said it hurt him to have her

out of his sight. He said he wanted to protect her, to pamper her—to devour her, she thought. He chose all her meals, even feeding her on occasion. He examined every curve of her body, every mark on it, cooing and asking about every tiny scar, every mole, every freckle. He sometimes made her feel like a large, well-cared-for doll, and it sharpened the edges of her life with him. In her life without him, she lived in a studio in West Hollywood that cost so much she ate ramen noodles when she could afford it and ate nothing when she couldn't. Her pride kept her from asking him for money. She wouldn't be kept.

The Poet took her all over the world. He wanted to do this for her—for only her, he said. She'd seen things with him, because of him, that she never thought she'd see in her life: the Nijo Castle in Kyoto, the Australian desert, the Taj Mahal, and the rice terraces of Bali. For the first time, she understood tourism's primal appeal to the human desire for ease. He was always the one paying, the one who booked them in first class or on nonstop flights. She got to be the one to demand drinks, not deliver them. To call for a bed to be turned down. Meals and bottles of wine and buckets of ice water and sunscreen would appear, as if by magic. She even learned to ignore the people who did these things.

The last trip they took was to Jamaica—for him, a four-hour drive along Jamaica's north coast, for her an eleven-hour flight that took her through Baltimore. Anaya hadn't been to Jamaica since she was a child, and the mere mention of that time filled her with panic. But this time would be different. She said this several times: when she packed, when she boarded the plane, when she bought herself a giant soft pretzel at the Baltimore airport. He had booked a hotel on the touristy northwest coast, nowhere near her relations or his. He met her at the airport, wearing a shirt open nearly to his navel. He was dressed differently somehow—his clothes rumpled, even slightly messy—and the hair, always so neatly combed whenever they'd met elsewhere, was unselfconsciously tousled. In this light, in the Jamaican midday sun, she saw all the ways in which he dripped entitlement. It lodged in the semicircular stains under his armpits, it clung to his hands so sweaty that the signet ring on his pinkie slid perilously up and down, threatening to come off entirely, and she could see it in her image reflected in his dark glasses. His whole life spent here and his body never took to the climate.

They hired a car to take them to the resort twenty kilometers outside of Montego Bay. The villas each had their own private plunge pool that looked out over the sparkling bay, curving blue and lavender and green across the horizon, the wireline between water and sky sometimes fading like a child's dream. Even if the villa annoyed her on some deep, even unexamined level, the beauty of Jamaica itself settled her. Her parents still called the island *home*—these thirty and more years after they'd left, as though the place where she had grown up was merely a way station, a stopping point on their meander back to where they belonged. Maybe she could better understand, finally, and so she got up early every morning to look at it, to see this unfamiliar part of the Island. No matter how early she left their bed, the sun was always up first.

"Close the goddamn drapes," he muttered, pulling the sheets over his head.

He slept until noon or nearly so each day. And when he woke, he ordered a scotch that floated to the room on a silver tray delivered by a Black man wearing crisp, white gloves. He had always done this on their travels. It was no different from how he had behaved on their other trips, but here, it made her feel uncomfortable. She didn't say anything, but she thought about it. Usually when he slept.

By midafternoon each day, they lazed by the pool, her skin becoming deeply gold and his becoming angry and raw looking. She had never seen this side of Jamaica: the moneyed, curated paradise. The total subservience, the smiles on the staff people's faces, a performance that, to her, looked like a contemporary minstrel show, but with Jamaicans obliterating themselves with burnt cork. Obliterating their natural way of speaking with British accents. The choreographed entertainment, the scripted good nature, and the young Jamaican men and women referring to the mostly white visitors from England, America, and Canada as *m'lord* and *m'lady*. Colonialism by another name. Tourism. Where servants could never be slaves because you tipped them, because they smiled.

Her family was not from this part of the Island, and her people, on the southwest coast, worked in government or finance. They were teachers and lawyers who had helpers and houses as nice as she'd seen. But this was something different somehow. When she pretended to be reading, she imagined the resort's employees in their homes at night, smoothing out crumpled paper bills, sticky with sunscreen, that had been pressed into their hands. Those dollars and pounds and euros worth so much more than their own devalued currency. The shame of it; the pride. She tried—tried hard—not to think about it, because these men and woman could be her family. Maybe even were. She had an aunt in Montego Bay, her father's younger sister. She'd had three children; according to family gossip each had a different father. Cousins who she'd never seen, couldn't have picked out of a lineup, they were always just called "Bethany's pickney 'dem."

That was all they were in some ways, a group of people out there, anonymous and unknown, who she was linked to through biology. And she was here staying in the resort instead of working in the resort . . . because of luck. She was not special; she was not of value. She was just lucky. It was that simple.

The truth was, it was hard to even imagine who those relations might be, to picture their lives, because all this seemed a million miles from her life even if the blood in her veins, the features on her face, and the slant of her shoulders connected her to this place.

Anaya couldn't imagine what her life might have been like had she been born to her parents there, on the Island, instead of in Canada. Not just to her parents, but parents here with different kinds of lives. If she had been born here on the north coast in one of those shanties that she turned her eyes away from when they drove in from the airport. Would she have been one of these bright young things? Would she have bowed and scraped and used her good looks for American dollars? She would be one of the people turning down the bed, making the coffee in the morning, bringing scotch to the Poet. She wondered if that was worse or better than what she was doing now.

When she tried to ask anyone on staff how they liked working at the resort, she was given an odd smile before their eyes went dead and flat. The answer was always some version of *It's not so bad*. And *It's work, and we need work*. Except for one kid who looked at her, saw her dark skin, heard something vaguely familiar in her voice. He met her eyes directly and said, "It's awful. I wish I could do something else. Anything else." He kept his eyes hollow like the others, his face smeared with that same toothy grin, as if someone might be watching him. And then suddenly a flash of fear lit his face and quickly, oh so quickly, he said, "You aren't a secret shopper, are you?"

She could tell then that he had seen her for a fake or a fraud. That the recognition was fleeting. She was simulacrum. She wasn't Jamaican. But she was never sure how they could see it on her. Was it the way she sat or how she spoke? She could never seem to act in the role of Jamaican. She remembered coming home from a party as a teenager, walking past her mother's bedroom softly singing a reggae song. Her mother was on the phone and she caught her eye to let her know she was home and her mother looked back and said into the receiver, "All these pickney think they know Home, but they all quasi-Jamaicans." She laughed in a way that Anaya knew was at her expense.

She wasn't Jamaican, but at the same time, she was. Because she was born in Canada, Kraft Dinner, hockey night, and soggy boxes of poutine were as much home as the crispy skin of escovitch fish ladled with vinegar, steel-pan drums, and cornmeal porridge. They all felt like home, tasted like home, but were not home. She was a tourist, too.

The Poet, for all his skin, for all his money, he sounded more like them than she did. Even if she looked to be their sister, it was him they chose to address, because—she could almost hear them think it—clearly, she was only some North American piece of ass. How could she understand a legacy of rape and revolution, of colonial rule? How could she understand that the Poet was more family to them than she was?

But that blood ran through her body, too, unseen. How could they not see it and why did she so badly need them to? It irked her more than she could tell anyone that they thought she was American, just like the other Black people who spoke in big voices, directionless, who demanded things and complained. So she did everything she could to speak softly, to ask for things politely, to say *thank you* and *please* when receiving things. She'd never done this before.

Anaya wasn't the only one, of course. There were other young Black women here with older white men. These other women acknowledged each other, certainly, and most looked American. She knew instinctively that they were from Texas or Los Angeles or Massachusetts. Americans thought they were regional, but outside of America they often looked the same. There was a shininess to them. A quality that made them look imagined. Their hair was always unnaturally long, their makeup expert, their nails cartoonishly perfect. And they smelled—a smell that, as a child, she'd thought was money, but she now recognized as floral soaps and a layer of musky perfume.

These other women didn't speak to her either. Didn't participate in pleasantries or casual conversation. When she texted one of her very few close friends back home, the one whose people had also come from the Island, about the situation, he said, *Of course they won't talk to you.* He paused for effect before sending the second text. *They're prostitutes.* And she realized that everyone must think that about her, too.

She and the Poet spent each day spread out at the large saltwater pool positioned right above the beach. From a distance, it looked as if each of the swimmers might splash their way to the horizon and fall off the end of the Island, fall off the end of the earth. It would make sense—a prophetic reckoning. The Poet napped or wrote emails on his phone, and she watched the men and women bring drinks while she flipped through the magazines or books she'd brought with her. The words kept running together and she couldn't concentrate. She found herself reading the word *peplum* over and over again, not being able to make sense of it.

The same woman had been working as the pool attendant each day. She was beautiful, and she had the long limbs and grace of the dancers Anaya knew from theater school. Her hair was a wig, but it suited her in a way, made the most of the angular features of her face. Each day Anaya watched her stoop to gather up fogged glasses coated with sticky, blended-fruit mixes that'd overflowed the top and sloshed down the sides. She used a series of rags stashed in a hidden box behind a tree to wipe strawberry daiquiri mix off the edge of a poolside table, making sure to do it quickly and unobtrusively.

Only then did she ferry the used glasses to a small bar just beyond the pool. The bar had a thatched roof. There were no thatched roofs on the Island. Concrete, yes, stucco even—materials that could withstand battering from wind, from water. Anaya's mind drifted to her father's house at the end of a long drive in the hills above Kingston. The switchbacks that led up and out of the city were lined with palm trees and brush. All the roofs fortified with zinc, as if a house, a place, could protect anyone against that which had already been stripped. Been taken.

At home she had a drawer filled with the smallest bathing suits she could find. Scraps of cloth that looked like they were held together with wishful thinking. She loved that when she wore them, men and women would look at her. She loved that when she lay in them poolside, the impossibility of the swatches of neon yellow and orange against her dark skin demanded that people think about her sex. But the Poet wanted her in things that covered, sensible one-piece suits with discreet cutouts at the hip. No one was meant to gaze for too long at what was his—envy was directed at him. Lust, at her.

By their fourth day at the pool, she felt agitated. On their other trips, they had traveled, moved around, done things. But the specter of his wife, his friends, and his family hung beyond the gates of the resort compound. He wanted to have her in his country, but he could not risk taking her into the country. Anaya felt the reality of the Poet's wife for the first time, as if she were there, lying in the chaise longue next to her, accusing her. She tied a pastel-colored sarong at her hip as a cover-up. The one-piece crew-cut bathing suit underneath covered nearly everything, its only concession to sexiness was the two thin spaghetti straps that came across her back. She walked over to the long, poured-concrete counter. The bartender smiled at her.

"Just one minute, ma'am."

She had wanted his gaze, just for a moment longer, anything to make her feel like she wasn't a whore. He turned on the blender, whipping up a batch of cocktails even though it was not yet noon. He handed a round of drinks to a sunburnt woman who spoke to no one in particular, her voice shrill and too loud.

"All the flies at breakfast this morning," she screeched. "Who knew there could be so many flies?"

"I'm sorry, madam," he apologized. He started to speak, explaining the flora, the fauna, but she silenced

him with one hand. She had the same overly pink skin
as the Poet. Her hat slopped shade over her face, but the
crown was cut out of it and a wiry tuft of hair peeked
out the top.

"They were on my children's French toast." The
woman went on: "It's unsanitary."

Anaya guessed she was from New York. She remembered the Park Avenue ladies who screamed at and
then dismissed her when she worked on the Upper East
Side. In the alternative version of her life, she *was* the
staff at the resort—the babysitter, the cook.

He had fallen asleep on his lounge chair. The scotch,
half drunk, would be replaced by another within minutes. From the bar, Anaya watched the rise and fall of
his chest; the skin was smooth and his graying chest
hair gnarled. Sometimes she could see bits and pieces
of what he must have been like as a young man. Handsome, certainly. She didn't struggle to imagine that.
What she saw now was loutish and, worse, she knew
at one time it had been charming. The way he made
a pretense of timing the waitstaff anywhere they went,
his wink, that smile he had where his mouth turned up
at the corners and he looked like he was going to laugh
and then, instead, he sneered. Would he have liked her
had he met her working next to the pool instead of in
the presidential palace? Would he have been so keen to
take her places, to travel with her, if she'd had limited

education or bad manners? Or would her beauty have undercut all that?

She turned from the thatched hut and waded into the pool where she rolled, floating, on her back. The sun was high and hot, and she imagined her escape from the Poet. She wanted to give him up, and she wanted to give him everything. She wanted to love him. She wanted him to love her. She wanted to be his fantasy, and she wanted to be real for him, too. They still had another week planned. She had no money—and no way to get back to the airport even if she could go.

Quietly, she stepped out and settled on a chaise longue, letting the sun burn off the water from the pool. She listened as a waiter across the way explained to a tiny woman covered from head to toe in linen about the national dish. Ackee, he said, was fruit. Cooked with salted codfish, onions, tomatoes. Poisonous if not handled correctly. It hardly ever was poisonous, of course, but didn't tourists like the potential of danger behind a nine-foot-high fence?

"A-key?" the woman repeated, pronouncing the word as though it were foreign, not English. It sounded the way Anaya had learned to say *here* while studying Spanish in her high school class.

"Ack-ee," the waiter said, pronouncing it again, slowly, as you would for a child.

"Ah-key," she said back to him with a smile,

convinced she had captured the word and held it in her grasp, like a monarch butterfly that might flitter away. "Did you hear that, Lachlan?" she said to the boy next to her, whose nose and neck were an angry shade of red. "We are going to have Ah-key for breakfast. Ah-key."

Why did this make her want to laugh and cry at the same time? Why did she hate the man taking the order as much as the woman ordering? Next to her, the young woman—the pool attendant with the midnight skin—piled abandoned towels in her arms. The back of her polo read *Director of Water Sports*. Two little boys that Anaya suspected of being Lachlan's brothers came up to her, interrupting her work.

"We need to get a present for my dad," the smallest boy demanded. "Can you help us?"

The woman looked around helplessly for a moment. She'd arranged something like a smile on her face when she turned to the children.

"The director of the Kidz Club should be here at any moment," she said. "Maybe she can help you?"

The older of the two boys rolled his eyes.

"But you're here now," he said. "You're just grabbing towels. Can't you help us?" He paused briefly. Then, as an afterthought, he said, "Please?"

The woman looked around, and there were towels everywhere. The morning swimmers had all gone to lunch, and the pool area would need to be immaculate for their return. Not finishing in time wasn't an option.

She gave the boys five Jamaican one-dollar coins she had in her pocket. Not enough to buy anything. What was the Jamaican dollar worth, after all?

"Go to the gift shop," she said. "See what you can find."

Five dollars Jamaican. Less than a dime in the States. What was there in the gift shop that cost that little? What could that buy? A stick of gum? One of those pennies that came imprinted with the date and location? The kind of stuff a kid would show off for a week and then lose and then, years later, find again at the back of a bottom drawer, fingering it slowly and then chucking it in a plastic garbage bag before heading off to college.

The woman was standing over her. "Another towel, miss?"

Anaya took one, propping it under her head, saying *thank you* too effusively. She wanted to say that she was sorry, that she shouldn't be included, too, shouldn't be lumped in with these Americans. She knew saying any of it was too much. Instead, she asked, "Do you think the boys will be able to find anything for their father?"

Anaya took off her sunglasses and peered at the woman, who frowned for a moment before bending over to pick up a towel Anaya had discarded on the floor.

"Maybe. Maybe not," she said with a shrug. "But money from another place can be a treat, nuh? An' beside, many of these people come here and never see one cent Jamaican money."

The answer was practiced. Anaya understood she'd given it before, had memorized the placement and order of each word because it sounded like a speech.

"It was nice of you," Anaya said.

"I want everyone to enjoy themselves here in my country. Will you be needing anything else, miss?"

She shook her head, and the woman left. She had missed lunch but she wasn't hungry. The Poet never let her order her own lunch.

"It's too hot," he said, waking up finally. "I'm going back to the room to take a nap."

She told him that she would be up soon. He meandered away, and she ordered a daiquiri from a passing waiter. She flipped onto her stomach, mashing her face into the towel that smelled of bleach and lavender and closed her eyes, feeling the sun beat down on her back, further darkening her skin just as her mother had always warned her against.

Anaya was pulled from her late-afternoon sleep by the shouts of the two boys. Their sneakers hit the concrete with enough force that she felt the vibrations up through the chaise longue. She opened her eyes, the pool area—as if by magic—had been cleaned and the woman stood at her post in front of a pile of freshly laundered and perfectly folded towels, her eyes wide open as the boys came at her at full speed. The larger of the two boys stopped only two inches from her. He was shorter than she was, but his bright red face and heavy, ragged breath made him mildly intimidating.

"The money you gave me . . . it's no good!" The boy pitched one of the coins at the woman's feet. As it hit the concrete, the woman flinched. He poked his finger into her face, his mouth sneering. "Liar!" he screamed. "You're nothing but a liar."

She put up her hands to shield her face as if from a palm or fist, and for a second, Anaya thought that the boy might actually hit her. When the blow didn't come but the child stood there quivering, the woman lowered her hands and leaned forward, snatching the child by the arm and staring directly into his ruddy face without blinking or saying a word. He stared back at her with a steely gaze, breathing rapidly, in and out. In and out.

"I'm going to tell," he said. "I'm going to tell my dad you're a liar!" He paused, then, "And that you hit me."

Later, back in the room, as she changed out of the wet bathing suit, some of the story spilled out of her. The Poet told Anaya to stay out of it, that these things happened all the time. That if the women lost her job, there would be another. And she spiraled, circling her concern that she was not enough for him, that she would never be anything more to him than a trinket, a gaudy bracelet, something pretty but cheap to show off to his friends. When she was used up or burnt out or old, would he simply be done with her?

She saw herself naked in the mirror now. He sat on the bed behind her, half of his reflection watching her. She could tell that they were both thinking it, that her body would not stay this beautiful. And together they quietly calculated what she was worth. He understood the math so easily and so quickly that he made fun of her, told her that she was overreacting about the kids. He told her that she didn't understand the way Jamaica worked and that she never would. He justified, or tried to. "These people would be unemployed without my money."

Yes, that was clear. It was his. Not theirs, because they were not a unit, not a couple. She was his. And then he pulled her to him and kissed her roughly—but not meanly—smelling of scotch, the stubble around his sour mouth scratching her cheek and above her lip. The light of the day was fading and a cooling breeze was pushing in from the bay. She wanted to get to the airport and get home as soon as she could. She wanted to get away from him and forget she knew him or that this trip had ever happened. Was it the beauty in the words he put together, or was it all that money, all those places he took her?

"Get off me." Her voice was low and clipped. "You're disgusting."

He pulled her tighter. "And you like it, don't you?"

He was right. She *had* liked it. She had liked the way her disgust made her feel. She had liked pretending to be his wife. She had liked being told what to eat and what to wear. She had liked being used physically. It was ugly, but it was true. All of it. Every last part.

She shoved him away. "I'm not joking."

He laughed at her. That same cynical laugh that told her she didn't understand herself. That he saw what she couldn't. That he understood what she was far better than she did.

"What about your wife?" she asked. "What about your family?"

He shrugged, spinning and rattling the ice in his glass, unconcerned. Outside she heard children screaming. Children, white like him. Children, white like his. Out of many, one people. Out of many, one of her. Out of an island diaspora spread to every corner of the planet, how was it that he found her, of all people? She was not at all the kind of girl to have a married lover.

She thought about getting dressed but stopped. Why bother? In the closet hung her clothing, her suit, smart, lightweight fabric, bought on a trip to New York. She wanted these items to suggest something about her. They didn't. They never would. She crawled into the bed and pulled the coverlet over her head. The evening sun made it feel as if she were at the mouth of a cave, and she closed her eyes.

She heard him set his drink down too heavily on the table next to the bed. He pulled the blankets back and folded himself in around her body. He extended long, slender fingers toward her head, reaching for the dark hair that frizzed around her temple. She opened her eyes again when he placed one hand on her belly, and then he began tracing the line of her leg up and up and up. She didn't look at him, but she could feel him watching her, his gaze a cool current under the warm surface water. His back was to the window and she looked out over him, toward the edge of the world, beyond the edge of the world, imagining that she could rewrite history, could leave him there in this bed to rot. But she knew that, no matter how much she wanted it, she couldn't remake the world, much less herself. And in that moment, she held in her mind those ancient explorers who feared they would sail off the world's edge and disappear.

The Cape

THE WELLFLEET HOUSE had been empty for nearly three months when they drove up after Neel's accident. Mina wasn't sure how long they were going to stay on the Cape, so they rented their apartment in Boston to some of Neel's graduate students. She'd been like them once, one of Neel's adoring acolytes who stayed after his graduate seminar on modern European history, then on into his office hours, and then into the evening for drinks and tapas on Newbury Street.

Summer season was over and the traffic minimal. Mina drove the whole way, missing three cops and saying one of her little prayers under her breath while she was going ninety miles per hour in a sixty. Her sister Patty had used the house last, driving up from DC, with her three kids, the new baby, their toys, and their dog. Patty had married a Hawaiian man and was one of those people who had sent an etymology of her new off-spring's name along with the birth announcement: royal child, heavenly blossom, star of the sea, beloved. Back home in Cambridge, Mina had hung the cards on her refrigerator before deciding that two weeks was quite adequate to celebrate a royal child and threw the whole thing into the trash where Neel dumped coffee grounds on it only an hour and a half later.

Signs of her nieces and nephews were scattered over the front yard. Twin dolls' heads and matchbook cars hooked on a piece of fishing line swirled off the leafless bushes. "I asked them to tidy up before they left," she said as she watched Neel take in the toys, the chipping paint, the overgrown lawn.

"And what about the boy you're paying to look in on the house when we aren't here?"

"I don't pay him much," she said.

"And how much isn't much?"

She didn't answer him but turned off the car instead. They sat there for a moment, unaccustomed to seeing their summer house in the winter, looking weathered and defeated. She brought the bags inside and put on music while Neel turned on the TV.

She made dinner and they drank wine in the living room with supper and didn't talk, just listened to the stereo playing Billie Holiday songs about stardust and love. And while they did, Mina noticed everything that was wrong.

The pictures in the living room left by the previous owners looked more warped and cracked than they had before. Prints of butterflies, neither her taste nor Neel's. In the past they thought they were funny and added kitsch value. Now they felt haphazard: the squirrel figurines on the mantelpiece, the spatula that was missing a quarter of its handle and the poorly painted watercolors that lined the stairwell. Why had they bought the house furnished? And why had they kept all this junk?

During other visits, there had been so much to do that the decorating had been the last thing on either of their minds. They spent their time at the pond, bought things in galleries in Provincetown, and ate Wellfleet oysters, slippery and salty.

This visit, getting the house in order felt critical. It would calm her. It would make the small cottage feel like home. Unable to stand being cooped up inside, she started working on the porch and yard. It was difficult at first. She had always depended on Neel to do everything at the Cape. He had mended the roof, patched the screen doors, and cut back the beach grass. He had never been particularly handy, but he knew enough about the way things worked to try to fix them. But now . . . well, now she had brought along a list of YouTube videos to watch and a stack of do-it-yourself books she had checked out from the library.

The first week there, she'd discovered that the books were a waste of time. They were so old there were no pictures showing her the things she was supposed to be looking for, and they used terms that Mina had no idea about. When she asked Neel, he just shrugged.

He shrugged all the time now. Shrugged when she asked him what he wanted for dinner, when she asked if he was tired, when she asked if he wanted to play cards or drive into town to see a movie. For the first time, he looked old. She noticed now that he was not thoughtful, not wise, not sophisticated. Just old. He gave up shaving and showering often, and he looked less and less like a college professor and more like the stooped and bent homeless man her parents paid to cut their grass at the community where they'd retired in Florida.

She worked all day. After they ate dinner in silence using the chipped plastic dishes that came with the house, she went walking, looking at all the other empty summer houses, waving at the locals who didn't know her. They gave her the kind of smile she guessed they reserved for tourists. At least that was what she told herself. During the season, there were other Black people here: nannies and cleaners, employees at the oyster shacks, and out-of-towners. She hadn't realized in the off-season how white it would feel.

Sometimes she walked until it was dark and watched the local families through the windows when the lights went on. Watched them eat dinner, or talk. Watched them turn on TVs and put away leftovers. Sometimes she would stay out until her hands got numb and her nose ached from the cold until it ran.

Then she went back to her own house where the only light she could see from the road was the eerie blue glow of the television where Neel sat, his leg raised to increase the circulation to the newly toeless foot. She waited until he went to bed. Only then did she crawl into bed next to him, his back already facing her.

Twice a week, she drove him to Hyannis for physical therapy. He switched from music to the Boston NPR station as they got down the Cape, and the voices that echoed through the car reminded them that they'd hardly spoken in days. She dropped him at the doctor's office and then went to buy an ice cream that she ate near the bay, watching the gray-green waves hitting the dark sand.

Her father's people were one of the first Black families on the Cape, the Jamaican grandchildren of freed slaves who came on Captain Lorenzo Dow's banana boats in the 1870s. Who settled in Wellfleet and taught their sons, who taught their sons, to cull the fish in the northern Atlantic the way they had in the Caribbean. To make a living out of what the ocean provided. They were Cape people, locals who lived there all year-round.

Her mother's family were those who summered there, like it was a verb. They were the white people who ate the fish her father's family caught. They owned places—not houses—mostly in Hyannis and sometimes farther up, near her grandmother in Yarmouth. They could map back lines to England. Until her mother had met her father in the sixties, two people finding each other and rejecting the way they'd grown up. How pleased her parents had been, each in their own self-righteous way, when Neel bought her the Cape house. He'd bought it for her, yes, but also for her family, who hadn't been able to afford their own place there anymore. When the taxes got too high, they sold their place and bought something in a gated community in Florida.

Her parents had been the last to go. Her aunts and uncle and cousins had already fled to Providence or New Orleans or Texas. Places with central heat and air where they could afford to live comfortably. The purchase of the Cape house had been a way for Neel to iron over the rough edges of their seventeen-year age difference. A way to help her parents forget that before he'd been her boyfriend or her husband, he'd been her professor. The house was a promise to her parents that he would take care of her by wrapping her in real estate. And for a while they all thought it had worked.

But when she'd called them in Florida the day after the accident, her mother said, "He's still like a child, isn't he? Why in the world would he get fireworks? He's a grown man for god sakes."

"I don't know," Mina said. She was still stunned, unable to put together the pieces of what had happened in any logical order, even as she said the words over and over again.

Her mother clicked her tongue. "This is what happens when you marry an old man," she said. "You end up taking care of them and wasting the best years of your . . ."

Mina hung up the hospital phone, laid it into the receiver, and hadn't called back.

When her fingers felt numb, she drove back to the clinic to pick up Neel.

"How did it go?" she asked.

"Better today," he said.

But he didn't seem to be getting any better. In the evenings he asked her to build a fire. She dragged wood in from the small shed in the back, stacking it in the tin-lined fireplace. Mina lit a wad of paper under the logs, hoping it would catch. He sat in front of the fire while she pretended to read in the nearby armchair. Really she was staring at the place where his toes used to be. What was left was covered in scar tissue and looked more like a leftover piece at the butcher's. One night in bed the stump brushed up against her and she felt like her heart was going to stop, like she couldn't breathe. She waited until he quit tossing and turning and lay still again. And then she went downstairs, feeling guilty, and made herself a cup of tea and poked the fading coals a few times.

That December, their third month on the Cape, the water heater broke and they were reduced to taking cold showers or heating water up on the stove for baths. Neel disappeared for a day with the car and instead of getting any work done, Mina paced the floor, worried something had happened. He was smiling when he came back; he'd bought a solar-powered generator and a book on water heater repair. He handed the things to her, one at a time, almost shyly, and ducked back into the house.

The silence was probably the hardest thing for Mina to take. She was a talker. They had been a couple who spoke endlessly, sometimes until late at night when they would both fall asleep in mid-conversation and wake up the next day ready to start over. He always told her that he loved the sound of her voice and she had loved his. But now words sounded unfamiliar, as if each of their voices had gone up an octave, the house filled with helium instead of oxygen.

The previous July at his family's place in Little Compton, Neel had had the idea to get the fireworks for Bastille Day. His brother's house in Rhode Island was always where they celebrated Independence Day. His family called the place a cottage, but the house on Beach Drive was more akin to a mansion. Neel's brother, his wife, their three children, and an assortment of cousins who came through periodically from New York or Pennsylvania or New Jersey were always there to stay most of July and sometimes into August. It seemed like they were all medical doctors except for Neel whose PhD was the punch line of almost every joke about work.

Neel thought it funny—a historian's idea of a joke— to celebrate French Independence Day instead of July 4th. Mina had never liked fireworks. Not since one of the boys in sixth grade had put a cherry bomb in the toilet at St. John's Primary School and the whole toilet cracked, sending putrid water all over the floor. Anything but sparklers were illegal in most of New England and she wasn't sure where he'd bought them. Later she learned he'd conned his eighteen-year-old nephew into a road trip while everyone else was at the beach. Four hours, through Massachusetts and into New Hampshire, the *Live Free or Die* state, wherein you could get almost anything you wanted.

He had set up the display in the center of the backyard and his family gathered around.

"I'm quite impressive with these things, you know," Neel said, stage-winking for his audience. "Childhood expertise." He pulled out one of the long matches they used to light the grill. "Now there, you, the stunning young girl up front. Why don't you pick which one we do first," Neel said, pointing at Mina.

Mina smiled, a true professional, and picked the one she knew he wanted her to choose, a collection of ten or twelve Roman candles bundled together in metallic rainbow-colored paper with the words FIVE SHOT PYRAMID POWER printed on the side and an image of electric silver flames shooting off a glowing gold cone. She would remember this later, when they were at the hospital.

"Good choice, dear. Good choice." He set the pyramid on the ground, struck the match against the strip with a practiced hand, and lit the fuse. The paper crackled for a moment, and then Mina's eyes followed as the trajectory of howling orbs burst into the sky and a mashup of colors exploded in the night, lighting up a haze over the wide expanse of lawn. And then Mina was startled by four or five rapid-fire explosions. She was confused. They sounded much louder than the cherry bomb she remembered. She wasn't sure where the sound had come from, and as the color began to dissipate, she stared at the sky, still seeing the image burned into that place right above her head. She wasn't sure if it was the wine or the colors, but she felt so calm. So calm that at first she didn't understand that Neel was screaming, or why. By the time she did, someone had already run into the house for a towel. "My foot," he said over and over again. "My foot."

The towel quickly turned red and someone called an ambulance. There was screaming and crying. She knelt on the ground next to Neel and they both avoided looking down.

"It'll be okay," she said, stroking his back.

The sirens blared at the end of the street and she held on to Neel more tightly.

The medics came into the backyard and immediately unwrapped the towel. Red. More red. When she looked, she saw a pulpy mass but nothing that resembled a foot. Neel turned his head, gagged, and then vomited into her hair.

They loaded him into the ambulance quickly. Mina jumped in behind him and the paramedic slammed the door. She'd never seen her husband cry, but the tears streamed down his cheeks and he said "sorry" over and over again. At the hospital they rushed him into emergency. She sat in the waiting room, her tube top stained with his blood and bits of chocolate frosting. After a while she couldn't tell the frosting from the blood and she let herself cry.

•

Summer was coming again, they'd been at the Cape house nearly eight months and the trees had just started to flower with tiny, tight pink buds, and she broached the subject of returning to Boston.

"How long can you continue on leave from the university?" she asked, poking at the broiled fish she'd bought at the dock that morning.

"I'm not sure," he said. "They've brought in someone to cover for me while I'm recovering."

By the start of April, the disability payments from the university had stopped. She asked if they had asked him to come back to work in the fall and he wouldn't answer. Without discussing it with him, she dipped into their savings to pay the mortgage on the Wellfleet house and called the graduate students in the city and extended their lease. She took a job at the public library across from the pond and walked to work twice a week. She learned to bake bread, planted a garden, painted the rooms in shades of blues and greens and grays. Neel spent most of his time watching television. He had never had an interest in TV before, but now she would come in from a swim or from pulling weeds in the yard and find him perched on a stool in the tiny cubby of the kitchen watching soap operas. Every once in a while, the old tone would return in his voice when he asked her about one show or another, but when she gave him an odd look, he would shut her out again and turn back toward the television.

As the months wore on and she cleaned and she cooked, she also muttered *asshole* and *fucker* under her breath when he gave pointers while she scrubbed the bathtub and cleaned out the pans underneath the burners on the stovetop.

And just like that, it was summer again and there were tourists everywhere. The New Yorkers invaded, making their drives down the Cape to Hyannis take longer and longer. They navigated gridlocked traffic on I-195 all the way down to Providence. The town was clogged with sandy-haired families in Sperry Top-Siders and polo shirts, little Daisy Buchanans and Kennedy knockoffs everywhere.

One hot and lazy day, when neither of them seemed to be able to sum up the energy to say much to the other, they sat on the porch drinking sidecars. She felt heavy. Weighed down. Anchored.

"Where did you learn to make these?" he asked.

The politeness startled her, the way he asked so plainly.

"When I was bartending in Boston," she said. "Right before I met you."

"Bars," he said, holding the glass up to the light and inspecting the liquid. "Disneyland for alcoholics," he said with a laugh.

And she laughed, too, even though it wasn't that funny, relieved just to laugh. "Would you like to cook out tonight?" she asked.

His face brightened. He was almost all gray now, but she could see pleasure in his smile and around the corners of his eyes. "That sounds great," he said. "I think my mother left a recipe for her chicken in one of those boxes."

It would be July soon, nearly a year since the accident, and neither of them had talked about going out to the compound on Little Compton. Nor had he discussed the nieces and nephews who wrote emails or texted, or the brother who called every week to see how he was doing.

Eleven months, and there were still boxes stacked in every room. Things from Boston that had come out a little at a time when she'd gone into the city to get new clothes, moving their life out there bit by bit. Inside, she dug through piles of cardboard to see if she could find the recipe. It was in the second box that she opened. She stood up, clutching the tattered recipe card written in her mother-in-law's old-fashioned slanted handwriting and saw her husband trying, futilely, to drag the grill from the garage. She was out the door before she had thought the whole thing through.

"Here," she said, sprinting down the back steps. "Let me help you." Her legs were lean and strong from her time outside.

He was slick with sweat and breathing heavily. "No. I've got it."

She reached forward, easing the grill out of his hand. "No," she said. "Just relax. I'll do it."

He let go of the tiny kettle grill and it clattered to the ground much louder than she thought it would. "Fine," he said flatly, and went back over to the deck chairs.

She marinated the chicken and lit the coals as the whole sky slowly darkened—the sun dipping low, the night moving in, the stars glowless. Mina waited for the coals to crumble and turn red. The marinade was an odd combination of salad dressing, turmeric, and curry powder. When she pressed the chicken against the grill with the tongs, little bits of fat popped and sizzled onto her arm. "The days seem to last so much longer," she said, almost without thinking.

"I know what you mean," said Neel. He turned the pages of the magazine lying open his lap. "There is something to be said for winter, for being able to hide away from the day."

"It won't be like this much longer," she said, and flipped the chicken. "Summer is almost half over."

Saying that made her feel relieved all of a sudden. By the time the chicken was cooked the sun had set entirely. She mixed him another sidecar.

"Thank you," he said without looking up. He had

been staring off into the blackness of the night while she lit a citronella candle, finished the chicken, and got plates and napkins.

"You're welcome."

They sat in silence for a long time while she ate and while he stared down at his plate. He still hadn't started by the time she finished eating. "When I was growing up, they tried to force you to write with your right hand," he said suddenly. "They said it was some kind of learning disability, that there was something wrong with you if you weren't right-handed."

"Did that happen to you?" she asked.

He threw the fork into the yard and Mina heard it land with a soft thud on the unkempt lawn. "I used to get so frustrated, I always wanted to find some way to just make my right hand work like everyone else's."

Mina wanted to ask him what happened eventually, if that had changed, if it made him love his left hand all the more. But instead she stayed quiet.

He picked up the plate of food and turned toward the house. "I'm going to bed. I'll see you in the morning."

She didn't turn to watch him but she listened to the thump of his heavy steps as he strained to keep his balance while he navigated the plate, the railing, the new familiarity of his body. When she finally went inside, he was asleep on the couch in front of the television. She cleaned the kitchen and then took a beer out onto the deck. The can was cool and she shivered, feeling for the first time the crisp bite of the cool summer night.

"I love this porch," he'd said when they first bought the cottage. "It's my most favorite thing about this house." He pulled her close, he kissed the top of her head and behind her ear, which she loved. "Let's make sure we sit out here when we get old and gray."

She remembered thinking—even then—that he was already old. He'd been a teenager when she was born. And he had already started to go gray around the temples. "Let's hope we're not in this house when we're old and gray," she'd said, turning toward him.

"Hoping for bigger things?" Neel said.

"I'm not sure," she said. And she meant it.

Later, when they talked again and again about that night on the porch, they'd said maybe that was the apex of their happiness and that things could not get better. Her parents had warned her against marrying him,

"He's Indian," her father had said, ticking things off on his fingers. "And he was your professor."

"And older," her mother added. "Much older. Three strikes by my count."

Back then she laughed at their hypocrisy. She told them that they had no idea what they were talking about. She told them that their love was all posturing and that they were failed idealists and middle-class sycophants. But she had forgiven them and they'd never mentioned it again until that night in the hospital. But drinking beer on the porch of their Cape house seven year later, her husband inside, asleep, disfigured, and angry, she wondered if they hadn't been right. Now she was thirty-four and that conversation seemed like a dream. She reached underneath one of the rocking chairs for her secret stash of cigarettes. She lit one and watched the smoke she exhaled billow into the night and then fade away.

She spent her evening looking at her phone on the porch, reading articles about a reality television star's divorce and what Hollywood starlets wear to the air-port. She read a story about a dating site for divorcées and clicked on the link to find page after page of men who looked so much older than her. Men struggling to style lofty wisps of hair. Men posed on motorcycles or fishing boats. Men leaning on granite countertops, their shirtsleeves rolled up to expose a swath of graying arm hair. But then she realized they were all Neel's age. This would be him when she left. That is how she'd thought it. When, not if. Not *if* she left Neel he would meet someone. Not *if* she left Neel she might end up dating those men, too. But *when* . . . *When* she left him would she still be young enough to start over? *When* she left would she find someone with no past, and only a future?

It rained steadily into the next day and the roof started leaking from last summer's bad patch job. Mina collected water in the pots and pans all around the tiny kitchen as the water dripped steadily into the house, breaking the silence between them that had become the norm. She went into the basement, pushing aside the boxes and the albums, all the detritus of their lives. Nothing was unpacked and, like everything else, the moisture had caused the books and the photos to start to mold. Soon, they'd begin to rot. Water always wins. She sat on an old milk crate thumbing through the water heater book. She didn't understand any of it. There was no way she would be able to finish the job on her own. She wondered how much it would cost to hire someone. Money was getting tighter and tighter.

She heard the phone ring upstairs.

"Can you get that?" she called out. She heard it ring two more times before she raced up the stairs. But the line was dead by the time she reached the phone. It had finally stopped raining, and when she looked out, she saw Neel down at the pond. His cane on the shore, he waded into the water, and her heart seized, worrying he was trying to hurt himself. She ran out of the house down to the pond and waded into the water. He knelt there, the water hitting him at his waist, and when she got closer, Mina heard him singing softly, and when she could almost touch him with her outstretched arm, she recognized it as a Whitney Houston song, one she remembered her parents singing when she was a kid:

So I'm saving all my love for you.

She almost laughed for a second. She didn't even know he liked Whitney Houston. Who liked Whitney Houston? But when she thought about it, really, it was sad. She dropped to her knees and matched her voice to his, chiming in:

Yes, I'm saving all my love for you.

She wrapped herself around his waist, pressing her face into his back. The pond smelled stale and old. There was something dank about it, not like the liveliness and salt of the ocean.

"I love you," she whimpered.

He didn't answer and they stayed there like that, singing, the water gently lapping against them, until her knees got sore and she had to stand up and get out. He stayed there, though, kneeling, singing the song over again from the beginning.

That night he climbed into bed next to her and she felt his breath on the back of her neck. Mina shut her eyes tightly and heard his breathing become shallow and rapidly paced. She thought he was sleeping. But he slid his arm around her and slipped his hand underneath her shirt and cupped her left breast.

"Sing for me," he said.

Quietly she sang a part of an Italian opera about a woman who accidentally kills her own son and takes another man's son and raises him as her own.

"That is beautiful," he said when she stopped. "What is it?"

"Verdi," she said.

She wished her voice was thick and raspy instead of high and light. She thought that if she could sing Neel the blues, belt out a Bonnie Raitt song or some Muddy Waters, he would understand better what she was feeling.

Mina leaned over and switched off the lamp, and when she did, he pressed closer. After the sex, quiet and passionless, she drifted into sleep.

It was dawn when Mina realized she'd barely slept. She lay in relative darkness for a moment until the sun crept into the room, lighting up first the collection of family pictures that Neel had arranged atop their bookshelf. Their wedding picture hung next to a portrait of his parents on their wedding day. Theirs was less formal and Mina was giggling and shielding her face from the camera.

The night of the accident, the hours in the hospital waiting room crawled along. Mina spent her time wanting a cigarette, a sweater, a cup of coffee. But she stayed folded into the plastic hospital chair, waiting to hear that her husband wouldn't die. And that was all she thought in that moment: *Neel can't die.* That thought was the clearest thing in her head and she repeated it over and over again. Because she loved him, he wouldn't die.

Hours later, after the surgery, when she had rubbed off most of her eye makeup with the backs of her hands and she was shivering, the doctors came out and told her the surgery was a success, that Neel could have lost the whole leg, but didn't. That they had saved most of the foot was a miracle, especially with the amount of blood he'd lost. She'd kept her face still.

"Thank you," she said to the doctor. "Thank you."

How had she been that naive only a year earlier? How had she been so naive that when she heard "in sickness and in health" in their wedding vows, she'd thought it meant nursing each other through a bad cold or food poisoning.

The fact of the matter was that they could abandon each other in a million different ways—because of a preoccupation with work, or boredom, or an ill-timed phone call with a grad student or a flirtation with a colleague. She had thought of a million different reasons to go. And only two to stay. Love and guilt. And when she repeated these things in her head, they didn't sound like real reasons but rather abstract concepts that had nothing to do with what she was feeling, which was that her life was over and by the time Neel did die, there would be nothing left for her. Her life was over at thirty-four, before it had even really started. And if she was honest, really honest with herself, she wished more than anything that Neel had died that night. That the blood loss and the nerve damage would have been too much. Then she could have wrapped it up neatly, grieved him, and at some point, moved on. And she hated herself for wishing it were true.

She got out of bed as quietly as she could. At first she thought she would just make coffee, maybe even eat a bowl of cereal. But instead she pulled out bread and lunch meat. She went to work assembly-line style, putting a slice of cheese, a slice of tomato, and one tender slightly wilted leaf of butter lettuce on each piece of bread. When she was done, she wrapped the sandwiches in wax paper and labeled one for each day of the week. Then she hid them behind a tub of potato salad. That way, he wouldn't find them right away.

Canal

———

PILAR HAS BEEN dizzy, her vision blurry for weeks, before her doctor diagnoses her with glaucoma. He attributes her condition to long-term exposure to tear gas during the 1964 riots in Panama. "But that was over thirty-five years ago," she says.

They are in a small examination room and the paper wrinkles under her. She hadn't expected him to stand so closely to peer into her eyes, and she smells the sharp mint of his toothpaste and the subtle piney smell that she thinks must be his deodorant.

Her doctor pushes away from Pilar in the rolling chair and leans back against the countertop, taking out his pen and scribbling onto his prescription pad. "It happens that way, sometimes. Things have a way of festering inside you and creeping up you when you least expect them. It's just the way we age."

He rips the top sheet off his pad in a way that feels like he is done with the subject.

"Just fill the prescription," her husband says when she tells him about the doctor that evening over dinner. Men don't think about these things sometimes. She thinks about them all the time—the small lines around her eyes, the folds at the corners of her mouth, the way that each time she looks into the mirror, it is her mother she sees staring back at her.

"There's a message for you on the machine," her husband says. "At least I think it's for you. It's in Spanish."

The message is indeed for her, and when she returns the overseas call, to the Colón Senior Citizens Home, the nurse has to repeat the woman's name twice before Pilar recognizes it as the name of the abuelita. She hasn't spoken to the abuelita in nearly twenty years. Pilar had lost touch with her after losing her mother and father within a year of each other.

"How did you find my name and number?" she asks the intake nurse.

"Señora Stiebel had it written in a little book next to her bed."

Pilar grips the receiver tightly, sees the room go blurry. For the past three and half decades, she has lived in Canada, cutting ties with everything and everyone from Panama.

"Someone needs to settle her affairs, and you're the only one we could find."

"And what does that mean? 'Settle her affairs.'"

"There are fees to be paid and the body needs to be . . . handled."

"One moment," she says, holding her hand over the receiver. "Can you go fill that prescription for me?" she calls out to her husband in the kitchen. She waits a moment until she hears the front door slam.

"And how does the handling work?"

"Someone needs to sign for her in person or else she becomes a ward of the state and we send her to the medical students."

Pilar pictures the abuelita lying small and gray on a slab while students in lab coats mill around her and poke at her with a scalpel. She tries to rub the blurriness out of her eyes. She looks around her den, the cozy wood paneling, the love seat she and her husband had bought the first year they were married, the framed pictures of their children on the mantelpiece.

"Are you coming, Señora?"

"Yes, I'll be there in a few days."

Her husband drives her to Pearson Airport at 6:00 a.m. He waits with her in line while she checks in, and he holds her hand until they get to the security gate.

"Call me if you need anything and don't forget to take the beta-blockers."

She pats her purse and they kiss briefly. "I'll see you in a couple of days."

Her grandfather and his brother had immigrated from Jamaica to Panama on the steamship *Cristobal*. Landing in Colón, they had helped build the canal and stayed for generations. When the canal was finally finished, they had gone to work for the United Fruit Company.

Pilar hasn't been to Ciudad de Panamá since 1965, when her family left after the riots. They had known so many families who had buried one of the twenty-two Panamanians killed by the American soldiers. They had buried her brother, Marco, then moved to Toronto, leaving behind her cousins, aunts, uncles, and friends. But a little at a time, they left, too, and now there was no one left in Panama that she knew. Everyone gone to England or back to Jamaica, Trinidad, and Belize. Like her, they'd married in those countries, started over, tried to forget.

She flies to JFK. JFK to Miami. Miami to Ciudad de Panamá. The moment she steps off the plane, the linen blouse she put on sixteen hours ago sticks to her back and seems to melt into her body. She feels the jungle in the air, even though she can't see it.

The nursing home is in a part of Ciudad de Panamá that she remembers as bustling. The last time there were shops, life, crowds; she'd even seen a monkey once. The taxi takes her down streets that look like the end of days. There are boarded-up and abandoned buildings, garbage, and rats. She understands why she has never come back. Not until she'd been forced back for the abulita who wasn't even her abuelita—just the hired help that her mother made her call little granny.

No one has forced her, though, have they? She's chosen to come. She has to remember that. At the front desk, she sees the looks exchanged at her Spanish, which after all these years sounds shaky. She thinks in English now. Dreams in English, the Spanish having floated away like the memory of her brother's face . . . which, like her vision these days, is blurry.

"There are some forms you'll need to fill out," the intake nurse says. "Have a seat."

Pilar sits in a cracked plastic chair. A salamander scuttles across the floor and underneath a potted plant. No one minds. The heat makes her whole body throb and she reaches into her purse and squeezes two drops of the beta-blockers into her eyes.

By the time the nurse returns with the forms, she is feeling better, but she is dismayed to see all the forms are in Spanish. She realizes again how rusty she is and it takes her far longer than it should to get through the questions. When she finally finishes, she takes the forms to the window, where she hands them over.

"Do you want to see the body?" one of the nurses asks, shuffling the papers.

"The body?"

Her knees nearly buckle and she racks her brain trying to figure out the right words.

"I can tell you how to get to the morgue."

"No, burn her," she says quickly before she can think of the word for *cremate*.

"Cremation?" the nurse asks gently.

"Yes," she says, "exactly."

It is all about the money, after all. The home won't take credit cards and Pilar reaches into her purse and peels two hundred American dollars off a roll. She slides the bills across the counter. "Is it enough?"

There is a pause, glances are exchanged.

"Yes, Señora," the nurse says, and picks up the money. It is so easy. Only two hundred dollars to settle the abuelita's life entirely.

"There are some things in her room, Señora. Would you like to take a look at them?"

"Yes," Pilar says. An orderly is called he and leads her down a small, poorly lit hall. They pass open doorways of rooms, cast shadows across gray people. People hooked to machines, people slumped in wheelchairs, men and women in dirty clothes staring at the ceiling or out fly-specked windows.

The abuelita's room is at the end of the hall. It is small and neat and has a dresser like a wooden box with dresses inside it so light and thin they feel like sheets of paper when Pilar lifts them out. She puts them in a plastic grocery bag the orderly has given her.

In the next drawer are letters, written in what she thinks is German, or maybe it's Yiddish. She is embarrassed that she doesn't know the difference. She sifts through them trying to figure out what they say, then presses them into the pocket of her purse.

The box on top of the dresser is filled with pictures—worn at the edges—of strangers posed in a stiff, formal way. Pilar sits on the small, hard bed and sifts through them. None of them are of anyone she recognizes. They are nothing like the snapshots of Pilar's kids. Her kids are grown now and in her bag are pictures of their birthday parties, graduations, bright smiles, and happy eyes. Pilar doesn't remember being quite so contented at their age.

Many of the photographs are of a little girl and a woman who it takes her a moment to realize is the abuelita. Pilar sits on the thin metal-frame bed and traces the outline of the abuelita's face. Thick strands of dark hair are pulled back to reveal a large smile. How can this be the abuelita—this pretty young woman with a Star of David stitched on the arm of her wool suit, her arms gripping a chubby-cheeked baby?

Shuffling on to the next image, Pilar is startled to see her own face. Her hair is pulled into tight pigtails. She realizes this photo was taken on el Día de los Reyes Magos, their last one in Panama.

A year before the riots, the man they all called Señor Kennedy had agreed to fly the Panamanian flag at all the nonmilitary sites in the Canal Zone, but he'd been killed in Texas before his orders were carried out. By January of 1964, both flags had been pulled down in the Canal Zone. At least that was what Pilar kept overhearing from the adults when they crowded their living room at Christmas and again to celebrate the New Year, drinking ron ponche. Eventually, their talk would turn to politics. But she was only eleven and when the real talk started, either her mother or her father would give her those eyes that let her know she should leave the room.

The day before el Día de los Reyes Magos, she stood with her best friend, Mariquita, at the edge of the locks and threw pebbles into the canal. The two of them watched the sailors on the big boats and tried to guess what was inside. Mariquita guessed sweets, pounds of ribbon candy, condensed milk to pour on ice cream, all the things her family couldn't afford to have. Going through the locks, the sailors on the decks stared at them. They yelled, "Banditos!" and ran away laughing and imagining that the sailors would chase them into the streets of the ciudad.

The abuelita was in the kitchen that afternoon, sweeping in slow and practiced strokes. She was from Kronsburg, Germany. She was inexpensive, said her father, who had hired her when Pilar's mother had taken to her bed. Pilar's mother had what her papa described as "the sickness." So far, all Pilar could see was that meant a lot of lying around in bed with the curtains drawn. It was her parents who had chosen the name *abuelita*, a diminutive form of *grandmother*, a way to give respect and hold it back at the same time.

The abuelita stared at Pilar for a second and Pilar waited as the woman fumbled around, trying to find the right words. "Something you eat?" she said.

She pointed at the refrigerator, her head cocked to the side. Pilar shook her head no and went into the living room where she spread her books and papers out across the floor, next to the Christmas tree Papa hadn't taken down yet. The branches were starting to brown and bristle. They would burn it tomorrow on el Día de los Reyes Magos.

On the onionskin paper the teacher had given her in

class that day, she traced out the shape of the country, colored the borders east and west a bright blue, and with her favorite purple pencil she drew in the canal. She drew the line deep and dark, almost tearing the onion-skin. She remembered her grandfather's stories about the ways they had cut through the jungle for almost no money, trying to finish the work the French had abandoned. Before he died he had always talked about going back to Jamaica, about seeing his family again, never realizing he would not see the Island again.

She pictured the canal the way she'd seen it, a long snaky path surrounded by green on both sides and imagined it colored purple, the big ships moving slowly through purple tides.

She started on the mountains with her brown pencil. In the kitchen, the shuffling broom made syncopated sounds on the floor as the abuelita hummed a tune she didn't recognize. The sound was annoying, made her pencil slip into the margins.

She left her books and wandered into her mother's room. The curtains were pulled and Pilar wanted so badly to touch her, to get into her bed and find that warm place against her. Instead, she scratched lightly in the doorway until her mother pulled the damp washcloth off her face and looked at her.

"Pilar?"

She seemed surprised to see Pilar standing there

scuffing her shoes against the door. One time, but not recently, her mother had threatened bodily harm should they become scuffed.

"It's abuelita," Pilar said. "She's singing, and I'm trying to do my homework."

Her mother's eyes were glassy as she squinted and cocked her head as though she was trying to see someone far away in the distance.

"Pilar," she said again in that same flat voice.

Pilar moved to the bed. Her mother's unwashed smell was thick on the sheets and in the air of the room. Her hair, matted and greasy, lay on the pillow, and the depths of her eyes matched the purple color of Pilar's imaginary Panama Canal.

"Be nice to her," her mother said, in the voice she used when company was present, formal but hushed. "I need her help right now. I'm not well."

Pilar reached for her mother.

"No," she said, pushing Pilar away gently.

Her mother put the washcloth back over her face and sighed.

"Call the abuelita for me," she said, her voice muffled underneath the cloth.

"But Mama, she's busy. She's sweeping."

"Call her."

Pilar went to the top of the stairs and called out in her quietest voice, "Abuelita, Mama would like to see you."

She waited a minute. She could hear the birds out-side and the Riveras boys running down the block chasing their dog Pablito. But the abuelita didn't come.

"She won't come, Mama," Pilar called over her shoulder.

"Then go get her."

Pilar went down each stair slowly, counting to ten before she would take the next step, trying to avoid going to the kitchen and seeing the abuelita's accusing eyes.

"Stop dawdling, Pilar. I can hear you."

In the kitchen, the abuelita was still sweeping. She was constantly cleaning the kitchen floor; even though it was rarely dirty, she swept and mopped it each day.

"Mama," Pilar said, pointing upstairs. "She wants to see you."

The abuelita leaned against the stove and sighed. She wiped her hands in the lap of her dress and followed Pilar as she darted up the steps, taking them two and three at a time, wanting to reach her mother's bedside before the abuelita could stop her.

"Ah, Señora Ana," her mother said when the abuelita finally appeared in the door. "It's good to see you again, thank you so much for all your help."

Pilar's mother explained that she would need the abuelita's help, especially with Pilar's father busy at the store and el Día de los Reyes Magos tomorrow. There was a lot of work to be done; there were cakes to be made, food to be cooked, and clothes to be washed for the feasts and the parties.

Pilar edged toward the door, thinking about the mountains she needed to finish. She wanted to turn on the television to watch some of the American TV shows before her papa got home.

Pilar felt the abuelita's thin fingers close around her wrist before she got to the door. The abuelita wasn't very strong, but her spindly fingers held tight.

"Help me," she said. "My Spanish isn't good enough for the market."

"That is a wonderful idea," Mama said as they walked toward the door. "Pilar is an excellent helper, Señora, excellent."

Pilar shook off the abuelita's hand.

They took the chiva bus downtown, the abuelita tucking the folds of her oversized dress around her legs and staring down at her hands, which looked much younger than her face, pale and smooth. Pilar could see the light blue veins underneath the surface, almost like she could touch them. Sitting next to the abuelita on the bus, Pilar could smell her milky, sour sweat.

Through the windows she could see the boys from the Instituto Nacional, on the corners of streets, boys about her brother's age holding Panamanian flags and cardboard signs saying *Panama Sovereignty NOW!* and

Gringos Go Home! Marco had told her about how some of his friends had snuck into the Zone to plant Panamanian flags in secret. It was Marco who had explained how the students from the Instituto were working with the Zone police to protest peacefully. There were marches planned up and down Fourth of July Avenue by the students of the Instituto. "But," he warned her, "if the government in the Canal Zone won't live up to Kennedy's promise, we'll make them." She had liked the way he sounded, as if he wasn't afraid. And she had appreciated how he talked about Panama, like it was theirs alone, and she'd felt proud of him.

There had been rumors that in spite of the ban, the students at Balboa High in the Zone were going to raise a flag sometime soon, regardless of what anyone said. Already, there had been a two-day vigil around an empty flagpole in the Zone. She had seen the pictures in the newspaper of boys and girls clustered around the empty pole on the wide expanse of lawn in front of the school in the Zone. A school she had never seen, even though it was only a few kilometers from her home. The boys and girls in the photos were a little older than she was. They wore white dress shirts and the girls' hair had been teased into stiff puffy balls. She colored in their faces with her pencil, turning them into gray splotches. Pilar read about the American parents bringing sandwiches and soda pop to the teenagers who camped out there for two days, insisting that school officials fly the American flag.

"What do those signs say?" the abuelita asked.

Pilar looked away from the streets and at the abuelita's face, which was tight and knotted. "I don't read as well in Spanish," the abuelita said.

And Pilar almost felt sorry for her. Almost. But she didn't know how to explain the words *sovereignty* and *gringo* and so she just said, "It says they don't like America." The abuelita made a little sniffling sound and clutched her neck.

They got off the chivas near the market and made their way in and out of the stalls. The abuelita picked up fruit and vegetables and studied them close to her face. She squeezed and stroked the skin, shook things next to her ear, and inhaled their scent deeply. Unlike Mama, she didn't haggle with the vendors and paid whatever they asked, as though each price were fair, even when it wasn't. It was as though she had all the money in the world to spend. She would take it out of the little coin purse, keeping her eyes on the ground and murmuring, "Gracias, Señor," so softly they could barely hear her. Pilar watched and trailed behind dutifully, rolling her eyes and watching the abuelita overpay. Pilar thought about stopping the abuelita, holding her hand back when the fishmonger and the butcher charged nearly two-thirds more than they would charge Pilar's mother. But she didn't.

They ran out of money before they'd bought everything that was needed. There wasn't even enough money to take the bus back. They lugged everything from the market in the heavy baskets.

After dinner they turned off all the lights to cool the house down and opened the big rolling shutters, letting in the evening breeze and listening to the city quiet to almost a whisper. In the flickering half dark, Pilar stretched out on the floor and watched *El Llanero Solitario*. Marco put up his feet, sprawling across the nubby fabric of the couch. Papa watched for a few minutes before he went upstairs into the bedroom and shut the door. When he came out, he motioned for Pilar to meet him at the base of the staircase.

"I won't tell you again," he said. "Be good to Abuelita."

She twisted one thick plait around her hand and made a face.

"I will."

"Did you let her overspend at the market today?"

Pilar shrugged her shoulders.

"When you do things like that, you aren't just hurting yourself, you're hurting your mama, me, your brother, our family."

"Sorry."

"I don't want to have to speak to you about this again. And don't you bother your mama about her. You understand?"

"Yes, Papa."

He went back up the stairs into his room and closed the door. Marco shut off the TV.

"It's late," Marco said. "You should get to bed, too."

She imagined the abuelita in the room they shared taking off her tattered old dress, talking in her weird language, crying softly like she'd seen her do sometimes, or even worse, singing.

"Can I hang out in your room for a little while?" she asked Marco.

"I guess," he said.

She followed him into his bedroom under the staircase. He sat at his desk under the sloped wall reading a book and humming "Love Me Do" under his breath.

Pilar sat cross-legged on his bed looking through his magazines. He had lots of *National Geographic*s that Papa got him for his birthday. On some pages the women wore no clothing, most were as skinny as the abuelita, but not as scary looking. Pilar stared at their bodies trying to figure out if they'd once looked like her and if she would eventually look like them.

All of the naked-pages were dog-eared and she flipped to them in each issue. One woman had countless spherical necklaces laced tightly around her neck, and her entire body was bare except for a thin strip of leather around her waist.

"Hey!" Marcos said, snatching the magazine from her. "Don't look at that, it isn't for little girls."

"Check this out."

He handed her another glossy magazine from inside his desk.

"The Beach Boys," he said, tapping the picture of four boys posed on a beach holding surfboards. "A new American band."

Pilar reached out to touch the magazine's glossy surface, to feel what was going on in that bright, sunny place, boys in crisp shirts, girls in brightly colored bathing suits, all smiling broad, clean smiles.

"Don't touch," Marco said. "It's Elmer's."

He was trying hard to grow a mustache and the facial hair came in patchy and light, making his face look more dirty than unshaven.

"How was school today?" he asked.

"Fine," she said. "Why weren't you there?"

"We were over near the Canal Zone."

She wanted to ask if he'd snuck in, too, if he had been with the group of boys she'd seen getting ready to walk up and down the avenue. But instead she said, "Does it look like America on TV?"

"Kind of," he said, "but different."

"Different how?"

"I don't know, Pilar," he said, shaking his head. "Just different . . . Everything seems too straight, so planned, almost like it isn't real."

He folded his arms over his chest. For a second, she thought he was going to kick her out of his room, and she would be forced to watch the abuelita get ready for bed.

Marco opened his desk drawer and pulled out a small map.

"Here," he said, pointing with the tip of his pencil to an almost invisible sliver. "This is Panama."

"I can hardly see it."

"But see how important we are," Marco said. "We connect this ocean"—he pointed to another large blue space—"to this one. No wonder the Americans want to be here. We're probably the most important country in the whole world."

He drew an arrow connecting the Pacific to the Atlantic using Panama as the center point. He took out another pencil and drew another line, from Panama to a pink country across the ocean. Germany. "And this is where Abuelita is from."

"How do you know that?" she asked. Marco never told secrets that easily. Like any good older brother, he always brought her to the brink of tears before he confessed, torturing her with the fact that he knew something that she didn't. But tonight, he didn't hold back.

"Papa told me," he said.

"But how did she end up here?" Pilar asked.

Marco shrugged. "Who knows? Maybe she was a Nazi." He held out his arm like some of the actors in the movies they'd seen on TV. "Hiding out from her comrades."

"Yeah, right," she said. "Nazis aren't girls."

There were about fifteen people in the living room the night of el Día de los Reyes Magos. Papa pushed the couch back against the wall, even though there wasn't any dancing yet. Music filled the room—45s that Tío Sergio had sent from Brazil spun on the record player.

Mama stood in the corner, supporting herself on the edge of the pushed-away couch, her red linen dress hanging on her like it was for sale in a store instead of on a person. She had combed her hair, but her eyes were still the color of Pilar's imaginary canal and her cheekbones jutted out. She sent Pilar back and forth between the kitchen and the living room for trays of tajadas and canastitas filled with ceviche. The abuelita was in the kitchen washing and drying glasses, refilling trays, and checking on food in the oven.

More and more people filled the house. Pilar stopped

once during one of her trips back and forth and did a
little shimmy to "El Tamborito" in the center of the floor,
flipping up the stiff crinoline underneath her pink cotton
dress as all the grown-ups laughed. Once her trays were
empty, she looked for Marco and found him sitting on
the back steps petting Pablito. She sat down next to him,
stuffing sticky, sweet tajadas into her mouth.

"What are you doing out here?" she asked, her
mouth full.

"Just looking at the stars," he said.

He got up from the stoop. In the faint he light, Pilar
saw the cut on his face.

"What happened?"

"Nothing," Marco said. "Get back inside before
Mama catches you eating yourself sick."

Pilar went back into the kitchen and the abuelita
filled up another tray. Pilar was about to head into the
living room when she heard the needle yanked violently
off the record player.

When she went out into the living room, Señor
Delgado stood in the middle of the room, panting and
red-faced.

"Those damned Americans have used our flag to
wipe their asses," he said.

Señor Delagado taught English at the Instituto, and
Marco was in his class. Señor Delgado was a good friend
of her parents and had been at their house many times,

but Pilar had never seen him like this. Papa wrapped his arm around the señor.

"It's okay. Sit down, have something to drink."

Her father motioned to her mother, who ducked into the kitchen. Señor Delgado sat down in a chair and her mother returned an instant later with a glass of water. He took a long drink and his Adam's apple bobbed as the water slid down his throat.

"What happened, hermano?" Señor Riveras finally called out.

"Our students," Delgado said, panting. "They went over there peacefully. They tried to raise our flags next to theirs. Tried do to what Kennedy promised."

His forehead was wet and he dabbed at it with a handkerchief.

"Those barbarians surrounded those boys—those children singing their damn anthem—and then dragged them from the pole. The paper said it was the other kids. But it wasn't the teenagers who dragged them. Those were men. Full-grown American men beating on our children."

The room was silent for a moment and Pilar could feel her throat clench up thinking about a man as big as Papa coming after her bother, who hardly reached his shoulders.

"They ripped down our flag," Delgado said before taking another drink. "We must retaliate."

There were murmurs in the room.

"But surely," Mama said softly, "surely this is a matter for the police and not ordinary people like us."

"Don't you understand?" Delgado said, standing up suddenly. "They've attacked our children! What next?" His voice got louder. "The fucking Americans . . . they tore the Panamanian flag and used it to wipe their asses and then threw it on the ground! We're good enough for them to steal from, but not to fly our flag."

Pilar had never seen a teacher talk like this and she felt a little thrill of excitement going through her.

"Already there is a crowd at the border," Delgado yelled. "They have already stoned the lieutenant governor's car. Let's wipe these people out. Let's take back our country from the imperialists! Take back our country!" Then he said it again. His voice got louder, becoming a chant, and then the room erupted with clapping. Her father slid his arm around her shoulders.

"Get to bed," he said. "This isn't talk for little girls."

Pilar kissed her mother, then her father, and went to her room. She listened to the noise of the party as she lay in her thin bed. She liked the way the grown-ups' voices would crest high and then dip into softer conversation. She tried to pick out her mother's laugh; it was usually the loudest in the room. High-pitched and tinny, it was equal parts charming and grating. It was something people knew her for, the way the laugh that came out of her tiny mouth seemed to overwhelm her entirely. Pilar waited for it, listened for the peaks and valleys in conversation; but she didn't hear a laugh from her mother or from anyone else.

She must have fallen asleep waiting, but it felt like only minutes had passed when she heard the abuelita slide open the door. By then the house was quiet. She heard the abuelita turn over and sigh deeply, she heard the low rhythms of her parents talking in the next room, and the hum of the new Frigidaire.

Pilar fell asleep again, but woke up suddenly when lights flashed outside her window and the abuelita shot up in bed faster than Pilar had ever seen her move. She heard the crash of glass and she clutched the sheets around her and curled into a corner of the bed.

"No," the abuelita murmured. "No, no."

It seemed like she heard the glass shatter at almost the same moment that her papa came into the room.

"Get dressed and do it quickly. The rioters burned the Pan Am building and are headed for the U.S. Embassy next. The Americans are coming through the neighborhood and burning anything they can. We have to go now! "

Pilar pulled on the party dress still on the floor of her room but couldn't find her shoes.

"I can't find my shoes, Papa," she called.

"Leave them," he said, "just come."

She and the abuelita ran into the living room, which was dark and shadowy, but the bright lights coming from the windows created shifting, scary patterns on the walls that made her feel like she'd never been there before. Her mama and papa and Marco were already there, waiting.

"Let's go," Papa said.

She wanted to ask where and why, but she knew better. Instead, she reached for her mother's hand.

"No," her mother said. "Not now, Pilar, not now."

Her mother pushed her back as they made their way down the house's still-dark corridors to the back door that led them into an alley. It was where the delivery people usually dropped things when they were too big for Pilar's mother to carry home from the market.

The alley was full of smoke and Pilar's eyes burned. She felt someone take her hand and looked up to see the abuelita's spindly fingers laced through her own, her face wan and her eyes frightened.

She covered Pilar's mouth with the sleeve of her dress, an attempt to protect her from inhaling the smoke as they followed Pilar's father down the alley toward the street. The backs of their neighbors' homes were already in flames and she recognized Señora Camacho's house cat, Cariño, walking alongside them, looking up every few moments, confused, at Pilar. She couldn't imagine how Señora Camacho had left her.

The night sky glowed brightly with the heat. She heard screams, and billows of smoke encircled her. She tried to find her mother's red dress, her father's white shirt, her brother's shiny, brylcreemed head, and all the while the abuelita held on tightly.

They reached the main street at the end of the alley before she was finally able to see her parents again, two feet in front of her. Papa held Mama with one hand and his Bible with the other. Pilar moved toward them, dragging the abuelita along with her, the streets suddenly flooded with light.

As she reached her father's side, Pilar saw her friend Mariquita running, holding her hand to her eye. When she stopped and moved the hand, there was blood. So much blood. All she could say, over and over again, was "Mi hermano, mi hermano." She put her hand back to her eye and took off running down the street. Pilar never saw Mariquita again after that day, but Pilar heard she'd lost the eye. Mariquita's family was out of the country two days later, before their son was properly buried.

What she remembers most though is what came behind Mariquita—that impossible flank of U.S. soldiers in helmets, with guns. It felt like there were thousands of them, shoulder to shoulder, advancing into her neighborhood and down her streets, stepping over or around the neighbors sitting on the curb and in some cases knocking them down. Pilar watched the soldiers advance toward her family, uncertain where to turn, their lives burning down behind the silhouetted men. Again Pilar reached for her mother, but she turned away, burying her face in her husband's chest while Pilar's father clutched his Bible to his chest and sang "Himno Istmeño" loudly.

The syncopated footsteps of the Americans, each dropping heavily, one after another, sounded like a tank coming down the street, and as they got closer and closer Pilar's teeth chattered. The abuelita pulled her close, her scarred and shadowy forearm across Pilar's chest like a talisman.

The soldiers broke roughly through the crowd and Pilar's face scrunched in reaction to the tear gas before she knew what it was.

She felt the abuelita's arms wrapped tightly around her shoulders. She clutched Pilar and in her funny Spanish sang, *"Alcanzamos por fin la victoria. En el campo feliz de la unión."*

Her eyes blurry, Pilar watched her brother, his small hand balled into a fist, rush forward half-blind into the wall of green uniforms, a speck against the panel of green, of guns, of gas. And then the abuelita was screaming. Clutching her and screaming and screaming and screaming.

•

Once the abuelita's affairs are settled, Pilar finds a bodega where she drinks a cup of coffee, standing up in the
back of the shop. She buys a packet of pivas and asks the
shop owner to call a taxi. The lavatory in the bodega is
small and dirty, but she takes off her shirt and washes it
in the sink anyway. She puts on the cool, wet linen and
her skin feels clammy underneath.

Instead of going to the airport, she asks the taxi
driver to take her to Cementerio Amador. The section
where her brother is buried is nearly destroyed. Most of
the graves are covered in weeds, and the grass is so high
in some parts that only a faint strip of gray peeking out
at the top indicates that anyone is buried there.

She hasn't been in the cemetery since the funeral,
but she remembers that Marco's grave is at the back, and
like many of the plots that surround it, it is untended.
Next to him is his best friend, Elmer, Mariquita's
brother. Both their families all but gone now.

She pulls up a handful of weeds from each grave
and brushes some of the dirt from the headstones. Her
shirt is already dry and she traces out Marco's name
with her fingers, pressing down each thirty-five-year-
old groove, wanting—even now—for it not to be true.
She sits down cross-legged on the grave and wonders
if she's done right by the abuelita. And she realizes she
doesn't know.

She'd had both her mama and papa cremated in

Canada, ashes spread by undertakers. Blown away. This stone, this place, feels so much more real. She sees a monkey dart from the headstones and she throws him some of the pivas she has in her purse, from the bodega, and clicks her tongue. Soon she will have to get up, leave her brother once again, and go back to Canada. But for now, she sits here, feeding the monkey, waiting for the sun to set, trying very hard to stay cool. It is hard to be the last one left.

An American Idea of Fun

PATRICIA'S PARENTS AGREED all too easily about her spending the summer in France. "It will help your French," said her father with delight. As though three semesters with a teacher from Ohio—who called herself Madame Roget even though her last name was Rogers—had somehow made Patricia fluent. "What a wonderful opportunity," said her mother. "Aren't you lucky that the Claudels are willing to do this for you?"

Yes, the Claudels were friends, and yes, they had three small children, but what had they really known about them? Her parents were dazzled by the ways in which they seemed so rich, so sophisticated. The Claudels were the only white family that her parents entertained regularly, even though they lived in a house in a part of Cleveland where they were the only Black family and Patricia had always and forever been the only

Black girl in her grade or her class or her school. The other Black families they mixed with were from their church or people they had known from Trinidad who lived in cities close by and who were also doctors, lawyers, and professors and also the only Black people in their own neighborhoods.

Improbably over the year, they had become closer and closer to the Claudels and their three small children. Each of the Claudels was half French, but they'd all had it bred out with a strong set of ruddy Midwestern features. They looked more like Idaho potato farmers, but with a name reeking of pretension. They spent the school year in America and then went to their home in Montpellier for July and August. Patricia wasn't even sure where her parents had met the Claudels, but from the time she was ten they had been turning up for dinners at least once a month. The day of these dinners, her mother painstakingly made recipes from a battered Betty Crocker cookbook and used the copper pots that hung in their kitchen. And she vacuumed twice.

Patricia had plenty of white friends. She rarely brought them home, embarrassed by her parents' lilting Trinidadian accents, the way the cadence of their sentences always made it seem like they were asking a question. On the few early occasions she'd had a friend over, they always asked where her parents were from and why they talked so funny. She stopped having people over.

She didn't want to see their eyes on their living room furniture, the sofa and chairs covered in plastic, each squeak against the covered brown crushed velour a tangible reminder of how her parents had come here with nothing and how they now had this big house in Ohio.

Two days after the end of the school year, her mother dropped her off at the airport in Atlanta and gave her a long-distance calling card and a jar of peanut butter.

"Just in case you don't like the food," her mother said, smiling. "I know how much you American girls like your peanut butter."

Fuck you, thought Patricia. You don't even know me. But instead, she said, "Thanks, Mummy," and put both items in her bag. She hugged her mother, inhaling her powdery sweet smell, then went through security without looking back. In Europe, she imagined she would be a different person, that the travel would be her chrysalis, and on the other side of the world she would emerge a new person.

Patricia had been brought up to dress a certain way. When she was a child people always commented on how fancy she looked, almost old-fashioned for 1985. While the little white boys and girls in her class wore jeans, or cutoff shorts, she turned up to birthday parties decked out in the stiff crinoline and starched white socks that her mother had chosen. Her mother followed behind her in a pair of smart slacks or a silk dress. She looked nothing like the mothers who greeted her in overalls, sometimes streaked with flour from baking a birthday cake, nails chewed to the quick.

Patricia's hair was always pressed. Collars always ironed. A wrinkle or a crease was a sign of lax moral character. On the plane, she changed out of her pleated skirt and Peter Pan–collar blouse into ripped acid-washed jeans and an Esprit sweatshirt. She jammed both the skirt and blouse into the trash, hoping to never see their kind again. As they sped over the Atlantic, she flirted with a British boy with pretty blue eyes and no chin who disappeared into the crowd once they landed. She tried to hide her disappointment. Most of all from herself.

Who was that girl? she wanted people to think, all of them, dazzled by her American glamour. She wanted to be the Black Jackie O. She wanted to be the Black Grace Kelly. Instead she felt ugly and frumpy and impossibly fat. On the train from London to Paris, she put on her sunglasses and pretended to read a book by Heidegger that the librarian had suggested even though she didn't understand a word. Later, when she remembers this time, she will see how pretty she was. A slip of a girl, really, long and thin in the way girls are at fifteen, and then, never again.

The French countryside slipped by, the fields of lavender, towns that looked as though they'd been put together with piles of bricks. And then she was there, the train from Paris depositing her in Montpellier's city center. Outside the station, the wide boulevards were scrubbed clean. Waiting for her in front of a tiny car, dusty underneath the blazing hot sun, was Mr. Claudel. She had never seen him like this before, his shirt bright pink, printed with tiny white goldfish, and unbuttoned midway down his chest. His lady-snatching threads, she imagined, and tried not to laugh.

"And so you've arrived, darling!" He clapped his hand, and reached out to hug her, which felt awkward and weird, both because her family were not hugging people and because she had never so much as shaken his hand. The *darling* thing was even weirder than the hug. He called her *darling* as they drove up into the hills, once even sliding his hand over the back of her head and down her shoulders.

The Claudels' house was a two-hundred-year-old cottage, situated on a bluff above the city. The dusty gardens, the moldering old barn, the cistern, and the clean, slightly salty air made her love it all the more. It was everything she had imagined France to be.

Her skin went from bronzed to dark in a matter of days. She took to lining her eyes in a deep kohl as she would continue to do for the rest of her life, and during her second week there, without telling anyone, she went into a French barber and had her hair cut very short, just like Jean Seberg in *Breathless*. Secretly, she was pleased that she'd been able to explain herself well enough in French.

The Claudels made her feel like an adult for the first time. They left her alone during the days with the children; three curly-haired children with what she decided were overly American names (Jennifer, Joshua, and Jack). Mr. Claudel worked in an office over an hour away, and some days, Mrs. Claudel worked at the small bookshop that they owned, and on others, she shopped or had lunch with friends. Patricia liked her time alone with the children. She sang to them and was a willing assistant in the construction of mud pies or tree forts.

Mrs. Claudel taught her to drive one Saturday and she picked it up quickly, learning to maneuver the Renault up and down the hills, stalling only three or four times.

"It will be better this way," Mrs. Claudel said. "You won't be stuck on this hill all day and you can run errands for me."

In the evening, even if she was worn out, she ventured down from the hills. It was a thirty-minute walk to the city center, up and down dark alleyways, and past the cinema that showed mainly American films. She'd never made friends easily, but a pack of girls called out to her one night. She approached the leader, a girl about her age but a foot shorter. She had stick-straight hair and bloodred nails.

"You are American?"

"Yes."

They gathered around her, peppering her with questions. They loved her hair. They wanted to talk about Michael Jordan and Michael Jackson. They told her stories in English and she did her best with her French. They mixed up idioms and she overexplained, telling them what it meant to "plead the Fifth" or when something was "old-school." And they told her what it meant to "avoir la moutarde qui monte au nez" or to "faire la grasse matinée."

They were mostly her age, but everything about them seemed older, better, classier. They smoked Gauloises, wore scarves, and seemed to dress almost entirely in slim black pants and pretty print dresses. They introduced her to friends and friends of friends, who had parties, who smoked hashish, who drank wine from gallon-sized jugs that they sipped instead of slugged the way boys did back home.

At a party, midway through the summer, someone, she won't be sure who, will put a glass in her hand and the room will get hotter and the party will swell as more and more people will crowd into the living room and into the cramped kitchen. Everyone will finally get drunk enough, high enough, and someone will turn the volume up again and she will feel the house music pounding between her temples. It will have a strange, grating melody, will not be danceable, but there will be something soothing in its consistency.

The boys will look at her strangely, as though they are unsure they know her, or unsure they are seeing her in the right place. And when the girls notice the boys doing it, they start to ignore her. They slide out of conversation with her and she is left standing alone and feeling abandoned.

She wandered into the backyard, feeling hot and stuffy. The conversations were rapid and quick, the daytime patience of the friends exhausted. Lulled by alcohol and desire, she talked to anyone who looked at her. She doesn't know it then, but this will mirror her adult life when she will drink too much at parties, drinking until she forgets.

In her memories, it will be much more romantic than it actually was. When she comes back from France, this is the story she will tell over and over again about the French boy. She will spend years describing him as a great love, impossibly handsome and cool. But the truth is that he will be a pretty ordinary teenaged French boy with a faint mustache, a cluster of angry red pimples at his temples, and a porkpie hat who grabbed at her, whispered to her in French that she was beautiful, making something tingle inside that felt exciting and powerful.

He said something to her she didn't understand, frowning at her, but the darkness covered the parts of his face that would help her understand if he was sad or angry. He put his hands around her waist, moved with her to the music. "Move your hips," he whispered into her ear over and over again.

She did the best she could, struggled to find the way she should move to the syncopated beats and eventually just gave up and shook her ass, the top of her head hot with embarrassment.

"Oh yes," he murmured, twirling her. "You've got it now."

Eventually he pulled her into a corner, rolled a joint, and shared it with her. Kissed her so hard, mashed his mouth so forcefully into hers that she tasted blood. It was an eventful four hours.

Just before dawn he took her into the smokehouse at the edge of the property. Even in the dark, she could see the shady outlines of pig and chicken carcasses hung from rafters. The sawdust shifted under their feet and the boy drew her in close.

"You scared?" he said, in a way that she assumed he must have thought sounded tender.

She shook her head no, even though she was both terrified and excited. The boy stuck his hand under her shirt, his tongue in her mouth and, to her surprise, all she felt was boredom.

This is the feeling she will always try to ignore when she grows up. But at the time, she kissed him back harder, trying to figure out what was wrong. They stayed there for a while, until she begged off, tipsy and dizzy and a little nauseated. Back to the Renault and down the winding hills as the sun came up a little at a time, illuminating first the red dust on the road and then the walled fortress of the town itself, and finally, as she sputtered toward the long pebbled drive of the Claudels' home, the ocean itself.

The next day she took a long walk with the children, chasing them around the overgrown gardens. Mrs. Claudel took them all into town to buy a raft of pastries and cheese, of jams in tiny pots and cured meats. She picked up half a dozen jars of cornichon and four pounds of butter before they all piled back into the Renault and made their way up the hillside. That evening the Claudels had friends in town from Paris. She was instructed to feed the children early and she put them into bed before sunset. Mrs. Claudel was not one to indulge in the type of French mothering that would ruin a dinner party.

The guests arrived in cars loaded with four, then two, then six people. Patricia greeted them at the door, collected an assortment of scarves and handbags that were tucked inside the pantry door. They hugged her, they called her "la petite negress charmante," and one man, a business associate of Mr. Claudel's whom she'd met a time or two, grabbed her ass, and then gave her a big wet kiss on her cheek.

She wasn't invited to the table either, so she ate dinner alone in her room, reading, but listening, too, for bursts of laughter, the clink of glasses, or footsteps on the stairs. Eventually, she fell asleep and when she woke up it was still dark. She heard the crunch of tires on the gravel driveway, the last goodbyes, and realized slowly that it wasn't yet morning. She went downstairs to the now empty kitchen. The sink was piled high with pots, the counter a mess of sticky wineglasses and plates with leftover pools of sauce and congealed flecks of butter. She would have to wash these in the morning. There was still a smattering of voices outside. She opened one of the pots, barely chewing before she swallowed the remnants of a cassoulet. The duck grease made her mouth slick and she wiped at it with the back of her hand.

She poured herself wine into one of the children's juice glasses. Out in the garden she stood behind a shrub and she watched the last of the adults migrate into the house for one last drink, one last cigarette before getting on the road. She was still learning to smoke and so took tentative puffs from the hand-rolled cigarette one of the party guests had given her. She sipped the wine, looking up into a sky so clear and bright, nothing like the sky she knew at home. She wrote, during this time, in her journal. She had wanted then to be a writer, and before that an actress, and later on, a psychiatrist. When the guests were gone, she moved into the space they'd left behind, moving the half-spent wineglasses and overflowing ashtrays to sit in one of the now vacant chairs.

"You look," he said, "like a garden nymph sitting here surrounded by beauty."

It was Mr. Claudel. He startled her and she dribbled a little wine down the front of the pink peasant blouse she'd purchased that afternoon while wandering through the alleyways of the city as she waited for Mrs. Claudel to finish shopping.

He sat in the garden chair next to her and stared at the night sky.

"I never get used to the sky in America, with all the lights ruining the stars," he said.

Below them, Montpellier glittered and she could see the outline of the old Roman aqueducts surrounding the town, holding it in from the rest of the world. She thought then it was like a fairy tale, like a castle with a moat.

"You see the aqueducts, yes?" he said.

"Yes," she said. "But I thought those kinds of things were only in Italy."

"The Romans," he said, "were everywhere."

She tried to imagine it. Roman soldiers with spears and shields marching through Southern France, but she kept picturing the mustachioed French kid dressed like a gladiator. When she thought back to this time as an adult, those aqueducts would seem more like boundaries, far less romantic, a way to keep some in and others out.

"The Romans were an epic civilization."

When he said the word *Romans* with his accent, it sounded like *Ramens*, and she had to keep herself from laughing.

"Are they very old?" she asked instead. She was playing dumb. Of course she knew the Romans were old. She was in Latin Club and on the debate team. She was the kind of girl who sometimes ate her lunch in the library. She wasn't sure why she decided to pretend.

"I believe they were built around 19 BC."

It wasn't until later that she figured out that he didn't know either. It wasn't until later, much later, that she realized how boring and simple he was, how little he knew about his own city. The aqueducts were fakes. They were built in the seventeenth century.

He took rolling paper and tobacco from his pocket. He rolled her a fresh cigarette and then one for himself.

"It's amazing that they're still here," she said.

"Beauty never fades entirely. It may be diminished, but it won't go away. The Romans knew how to make things that were both beautiful and functional."

She liked the way he spoke, the way he tossed things like this out offhand. He lit both cigarettes and handed her one.

"Are you having a nice summer?" he asked her.

"Very nice," she said. "And educational."

It was something her parents had trained her to say, and Mr. Claudel laughed.

"It shouldn't be educational. You are young, and you need to have fun."

"I guess," she said.

At age forty, with her therapist, she tries to figure out what really happened that summer and starts to realize that his idea of "fun," in its very French way, would be the excuse he used for everything that happened from then on. When he spirited her away to the beach, took her to a wonderful restaurant, bought expensive dresses she would never wear again, and when he finally came to her bed.

But that night she wasn't sure what he meant. She took a drag off the cigarette and accidentally inhaled, the smoke stinging her throat and making her eyes water. She coughed hard and Mr. Claudel came over from his chair and patted her on the back. "Be careful," he said. "And don't let your parents know that we let you smoke. Or drink, for that matter. "

He sat next to her on the grass instead of going back to the other chair. It felt nice to have him at her feet, to sit above him. There was something about looking down that made her feel like she was in control. It made her feel like she was in charge. Even though later she will understand that she never was.

"I'm so glad you could come. Every young girl should have the chance to go abroad. And Martine really needed the help this summer."

He got quiet again and she tried to think of something to say, something to talk about that made her sound grown-up. "I've really liked all the walking and the shopping here. I feel like I've lost a ton of weight just walking to the market and back."

They stopped talking and she could hear the chirp of cicadas in the trees.

"Did you know," he said finally, "that you can exercise your abdomen just by holding your breath?"

"That can't be true."

"Oh yes," he said, getting very animated. "I've read all about it. They've done these tests at the American University in Paris, where they show that holding your breath, if done correctly, can actually strengthen the abdominal wall. Make it stronger. Let's hold our breath for a moment. Let's see if we can feel it."

They were quiet for a minute, until finally she exhaled in a dramatic puff, and Mr. Claudel smiled and exhaled slowly.

"Did you feel it?" he asked.

"Kind of," she said. Mostly her lungs and her cheeks burned. She'd wanted to best him.

"You must not be doing it correctly. Here. Stand up."

He got up and came around behind her and put his hand on her abdomen.

"Hold your breath," he said.

She sucked in and she felt the warm weight of his hand on her stomach.

"Hold it as long as you can."

She felt the tightening of her stomach muscles and the pressure of his hand became more firm. She could feel the muscles in her stomach flex and tighten, and she heard Mr. Claudel's breathing quicken.

"Okay," he said. "Breathe out."

She exhaled in a rush just as Mrs. Claudel came out into the yard, and Mr. Claudel let go of her quickly and stepped back, putting his hands on his hips.

"Did you feel the difference?" he asked curtly.

"Yes," she said. "I did."

In her twenties, when Mr. Claudel emails her after he has met one of her boyfriends at her parents' house or seen pictures from her trip to Mexico with her girl-friends, he always sends her the same message: *This is an American idea of fun.* That phrase more than anything else makes her feel ashamed.

She is barely out of college when she meets a self-proclaimed communist at a bar on the east side, where all the kids from Brown hang out and talk politics or trust funds. The communist has a soft smile that could make anyone give up capitalism. She is drinking white wine and flipping through a catalog, trying to ignore the loud music when he approaches her.

"Catalog?" he asks.

"Mmmhmm."

He looks past her arms at the step stool for a dog, the toaster that cooks hot dogs, and the seat warmers.

"Tools of the wealthy," he says.

Her features are sharp, with edges like cut glass. She no longer has any of the softness that makes some women cute. She isn't cute. She is beautiful and that beauty—when she executes it—can be intimidating.

The communist's name is Brad, and she tells him that it is a dumb name for a communist. That the name itself is reminiscent of Izod shirts and date rape drugs. Later, she would tell her girlfriends that he has what look like "violation eyes." The kind of eyes that can see right through you. The kind of eyes that wouldn't let her get up and walk away.

The bar starts to clear out and even though he is talking her ear off, even though her glass has been empty for quite some time, he doesn't offer to buy her a drink. The college students are replaced by the nighttime Euro trash that seem to love the place, buying expensive wine as though America is just one big Kmart blue-light special.

When they speak about beauty they split it into the physical and the emotional. Brad says there are "merits of womanhood," a phrase that makes her want to puke and which according to Brad gives her gender a predilection for egalitarianism. And she pushes back, telling him that he must not know women. Brad the communist shrugs it off as though capitalism has made her immune to understanding. He drinks tepid water with a soggy bit of lime floating on the scummy surface, a water supply long ago tainted by the mills and the factories that ruined Providence before it ruined itself.

"And why do you come to bars if you don't drink?" she hears herself asking.

"The bars are the consolation of the oppressed worker," he says. "His only respite, his only comfort." This bar is not a workingman's bar, this bar is all slickly polished stools and chrome. He sells the *Daily Worker* on campus and downtown at the train station. Brown students will press money into his hand on a dare or as a joke, and he makes a living of it. Still, she wonders what he is doing in a place like this. Where everything is expensive, where everyone is oppressive.

"Know your enemy," he says. When the communist takes her home he takes off all her clothes before he takes off his own. He stops and stares for a moment, making her feel embarrassed, so she moves her hands to hide herself. But the communist gently lifts her hands away from her breasts and places them on his own shoulders and then he undresses.

He made love with slow and practiced hands but it was as though he'd gleaned all his moves from an R&B song. Patricia wanted to laugh at his caress. It seemed utterly ridiculous to feel his hands on her body and listen to the croon of instructions in her ear as he told her to move this way or that.

After that first night in Brad the communist's alarming gaze (like he can see her through her act), she is unable to decide if he is sexy or scary. She finally lands on the idea that he is a little of both. Patricia send him a one-word text: *Hi*. A few moments later he texts back: *Drinks tonight?*

She is working, and she answers two client emails before she responds.

Sure, 6pm.

While dating Brad the communist, she will feel both proud and ashamed. She will start to quote Marx and she will never let Brad meet the Claudels or her parents. Eventually Brad will get a real job and take some money from the parents who are of course very wealthy. That was how it was in those post-college years when everyone was trying things on and then rejecting them. The pretense of communism will continue, of course, mostly through a subscription to the *Daily Worker*. But he is on a management track. Five years pass before she even knows it. She finds herself telling her friends that he is her future husband. Wink wink, nudge nudge. The future perfect is always more interesting than the present complicated.

Toward the end, she spends a lot of time waiting for him, listening to excuses for missed dinners or movies. He is cheating, probably with the kind of girl who owns more than one pair of sweatpants, who gets her hair cut in a shopping mall. She will find digital pictures of the woman in various states of polyester-undress. This woman, really? This slave to capitalism? It was disappointing in more ways than one.

She starts to spend entire nights away from the house. She meets a new set of girlfriends and stays out until 4:00 a.m., 5:00 a.m., 6:00 and 7:00 even.

He isn't fazed. Takes it all in stride, says he is glad she is having fun. She snorts coke with clients, she palms the ass of her friend's teenage son, she puts a laxative in Brad's coffee, and she feels nothing. These things she does to jar herself out of her life don't work.

One early evening Patricia sits on the stoop recovering from a hangover, enjoying the breeze on her face.

The little girl from next door walks over and with a kind of world-weariness plops herself down next to her. She's met the little girl once before. She can't remember if her name is Karen or Kristin. She is wearing clean shorts and a T-shirt with stained remnants of what look like Kool-Aid and mustard.

"Have you seen Jason?" the little girl says by way of greeting.

"I don't know who Jason is," she answers. She checks her watch again. He is over an hour late. She thinks about leaving and wonders if he would notice.

The little girl looks at her pityingly. She is cute in the way ugly children sometimes are, her features a little too large for her tiny head. Her mother has plaited her hair far too tightly, pulling back the features of her face and making her look like a child who has recently had a poorly done face-lift. The little girl will be a striking woman when she gets older, but now she is just odd looking.

"Can I come in?" the little girl asks. "I want to see if your house looks different than mine."

It is nearly winter and the last of the late-afternoon sun has long since dipped below the horizon. Patricia considers what it means to be the childless couple who let small children into their condo after dark. What type of person does that? she wonders.

"Okay," she says. "But just for a second."

Brad, who is performing less and less like a communist every day, has chosen this place. Brad who she imagines right this second is putting his hand on some young girl's stomach, whispering in that girl's ear instructions about how to breathe. Or correcting her posture. Or explaining that some young girl's Zara dress makes her a cog in the wheel of the capitalist conspiracy before depositing that young girl's fifteen-dollar dress on the floor.

There are women she meets at his office parties who won't look her in the eye. There are interns who say that they are excited to meet her and disappear before they can even begin a conversation. And she knows that she was once them and that she is now Mrs. Claudel, who never looked at Patricia the same way after that summer, never invited her back to France. By the time she takes the little girl inside it is already dark. With no lights on, the condo feels colder than normal. The fluorescent lights reflect off the newly purchased stainless-steel appliances, the granite countertops they haven't used for anything other than a surface on which to do lines of coke, and she thinks again about why she let the little girl in the house. She doesn't know what she is doing.

"Don't you have any toys?" the girl asks.

"No."

The little girl walks all around the apartment. She opens cabinets and drawers and Patricia just lets her.

She sits on the couch in the living room while the girl looks under beds, in closets, pulls things out and examines them. The girl finally comes into the living room and sits next to her on the couch.

"You really don't have any toys," she says with a sigh.

It's after seven now, and she still hasn't heard from him. She doesn't know yet that this will be it, that after this night, things will be over between them.

"Do you have any cookies at least?"

"No."

There isn't any food in the house at all. Nothing to eat, nothing to cook with, lots of paper plates and take-out menus but that is all. She wants, all of a sudden, to get the little girl out of the house so she can pull apart his closet like she's done so many nights before, searching for a note, a receipt, something she hasn't even thought of yet.

The little girl sighs.

"You don't have anything good."

It's true. She doesn't have anything good. She isn't anything good. She wants to tell this little girl that there isn't anything good about this being a grown-up woman, that she should try to stay young as long as possible. She wants to tell her not to rush men or boys. She wants to tell her to avoid them at all costs if possible. But it isn't possible. It won't work. It never has.

When he gets home things will be broken. When he

gets home she will be screaming. When he gets home she will be broken. Not by him, but in spite of him. It isn't pretty, but men love hysterical beauty and he will beg her to stay.

Some People

THE PLANNING MEETING for International Day is on
a Thursday afternoon when most people have work. But
in Upper Montclair, Kerry and the other mothers (and
two fathers) that Lydia, the PTA president, has cor-
ralled look like a summit for the United Nations. Kerry
isn't sure she has ever seen this many brown people in
Upper Montclair. Certainly not at Goldenrod Academy.

Kerry and Nathan had chosen Goldenrod Academy
because of its strong academic program and the bro-
chure's promises of an educational model attending to
the whole child, physically, academically, and emotion-
ally. At least that's what they said to people. The truth
was, Kerry had never really thought that much about
schools. Ever.

Kerry's parents immigrated to New York from Jamaica before she was born. Her older sisters were both

born on the island, so Kerry was the only natural-born American in the family. She'd grown up in Queens Village, always around Jamaicans and the children of Jamaicans, and she thinks of herself as a city girl. This part of New Jersey, though just an hour from the city, feels like the country. It feels like another planet, even. It's all so clear, so manicured.

When she got pregnant she had figured that they would find a place in the city, either public or private, but Nathan had gone to a public school in the South Bronx where he remembered moldy textbooks and teachers too tired to do much more than turn on a filmstrip. Goldenrod had been one of the reasons they moved in the first place.

The campus is in the former building of a for-profit college on the outskirts of Upper Montclair. The front is floor-to-ceiling glass. Ten years earlier, when the building went into foreclosure, the board of Goldenrod Academy bought the place at auction. It was a good deal. But it still looks more like a bank than a school, the ceiling slanting at a particular architectural angle that lets in a lot of sunlight.

Kerry sits with the other parents in a semicircle in the back of the cafeteria in plastic chairs that look nicer than the ones she'd had at her wedding. You had to make a certain amount of money to send your kids to Goldenrod. Sure, there were scholarships, but even the families who got those were middle class, would be wealthy, even, in some other parts of the country.

It is Nathan's money, of course. Kerry hasn't really worked since she was pregnant with Lady, when it seemed silly to keep bringing people coffee or making travel reservations when she could spend time parenting and taking care of Lady and working on the writing career she insisted she wanted. At least, that was the way Nathan had framed it when he had suggested Upper Montclair and this life. She was temping then, that end-of-week paycheck with a gut punch of taxes taken out of the measly eleven dollars an hour she was getting. The ignominy of having to go over the time card a supervisor had signed off on after she realized one week that she hadn't been paid for the promised overtime. She hated these things, the way they'd made her feel. When she thought about them now, it seemed like another life.

Nathan's mother had worked when he was growing up. Nathan was left with neighbors or aunties, or whoever else would keep him and Darius out of the streets in those hours between the end of the school day and when his mother might make it home. Nathan likes to be hands-on. Nathan, who grew up without a father, who works at home, who seems to spend most of his time thinking about what will make Lady happy, takes on much more than she does. Nathan has learned to braid Lady's hair, to fix her lunch, to pick out school clothes. When Kerry tries to make lunch for Lady it always ends up wrong. Fruit Roll-Ups and a banana, which Lady won't eat because it is too much fruit. Another time, Kerry makes two sandwiches instead of putting in a snack when she can't find one in the pantry.

The handout Lydia gives is almost four pages, double-sided. It has lists of different allergies: gluten, tree nuts and peanuts, wheat and soy and MSG. Things she never knew people could have allergies to, like sunlight, or fruit.

"International Day is, like, it's a chance for our kids to learn a little more about the world. As you know, one of the key principles here at Goldenrod is diversity. We want our kids to be citizens of the world."

She tries to imagine then what Lydia's idea of diversity might be, and she wonders if it might mean visiting the part of the Bronx where Nathan grew up, all of an hour away from Upper Montclair. She almost laughs thinking about Lydia navigating sidewalk street vendors or going into African hair-braiding salons.

Lydia looks skyward, looking like she's trying to run some numbers in her head. "Let's see. Each of you needs enough for, like, about two hundred bites." She pauses. "Last year, the Caloza family made a huge pot of sinigang soup and just gave everyone a mouthful in Dixie cups."

Drinking hot soup out of a Dixie cup sounds like a horrible way to spend an afternoon, but Kerry scribbles 200 *bites* into her notebook.

After the presentation, Lydia makes a beeline for her.

"I keep trying to catch you," Lydia says, nibbling at a cookie but somehow seeming not to eat it. "But you are a hard one to catch up with. I hardly ever see you at pickup or drop-off. I always see that handsome husband of yours!"

"I work," Kerry says. "A lot."

She gathers her coat, hoping the conversation will be quick, that she can get home and watch movies in bed while she pretends to be writing.

"What do you do?" Lydia asks, her eyes suddenly bright.

"I'm a writer," Kerry says. She can't remember the last time she's said that aloud. But she can't remember the last time she was asked either. When she met the other mothers, they never asked. For five years now, she's just been *Lady's Mom*. She fiddles with the edge of her sweater; she wonders how she can make what she is about to say sound true. Or maybe if she says it with conviction, it will be real.

"I write screenplays," Kerry says. "Mostly comedies, sometimes TV shows."

This isn't true exactly. When she was in her twenties, she'd interned for a late-night TV show host and then worked as a script assistant on a sitcom that was canceled after one season. It was a terrible show. Everyone involved understood this.

This screenplay is the first she's ever written on her own. The character is like the person she would be if she didn't have this life. Like her in New York before she met Nathan. Except that the character is white. And the character has a great job in publishing. Darius keeps sending her ideas for the adorable mishaps that the character gets into: bad blind dates, men who call too much, being overly honest in a work meeting. The setups are funny, but they always fall flat when she tries to make them work. What does she know about being funny anyway? She spends her days talking about homemade-cupcake recipes, and who dresses her children in bespoke clothes.

"How interesting," Lydia says like she means it.

Lady had started first grade that fall, and Kerry wanted to make a good impression. She wanted to show that she was a parent who was there and involved. At the first meeting, Lydia had said just that. *We need parents who are here! Parents that care! Parents who will make Goldenrod Academy grow!*

Kerry could practically see the exclamation points hanging in the air when she said it. And so at the parents' opening assembly, she'd held her hand up too quickly because she wanted—desperately—to be a better parent to Lady.

"Six committees?" Nathan said over dinner the night after the opening assembly. "Six?"

"I'm trying," she'd said. "I'm trying to be a more involved mom."

He raised his eyebrows. "Okay. Do the damn thing."

They were eating takeout from the containers again, and, as usual, she was feeling vaguely ashamed about it. Nathan's mother would never order takeout. Her mother would never order takeout. But here they were for the third time this week (the *third!*), and all she could hear was her mother's voice saying, *Some people just don't care about what they eat, about the health and nutrition of their families.*

Some people always proceeded some deeply held judgment. It meant that whatever action was being described was deeply, inherently wrong and callous and indicative of what trash that person really was. Growing up, she'd heard: *Some people think they can call your house anytime, day or night.* Or *Some people think that they don't need to talk to adults with the respect they'd give a house cat.* Or *Some people just keep their house any old way, yuh see?* When she'd tried to work the line into her brief attempt at stand-up, she took on her mother's posture: neck held overly straight, her face turned up with narrowing eyes and an expression that was a little haughty. She mimicked her mother's Jamaican accent and the way she had of looking down her nose, both literally and figuratively. The performance was a little bit English, the way she knew some Jamaicans to be, the way they adopted English affectations, the way they liked to act like Jamaica wasn't just another boat stop in the slave trade. The way they indicated that the Island was better than every other place in the world. But no one ever laughed, because no one ever understood what she was trying to do. Growing up, these warnings, these nebulous people, they were the people she was *not* supposed to be like. These *some people* constituted unvarnished instruction.

The other parents had retreated into the rest of their Thursday afternoon, but Kerry could not find a way out of her conversation. "I'm so glad you came," Lydia says, looping her arm through Kerry's. "Did that all make sense?"

Kerry nods.

"I just love making new mommy-friends who might have experience with other parts of the world," Lydia says, stacking up the extra handouts. Kerry thinks for a second about helping her, but she worries if she does, she will be stuck even longer.

"I'm not from another part of the world," Kerry says. "I'm American."

Kerry watches as the red creeps up Lydia's face and spreads to her cheeks.

"Well, of course you are," she says, squeezing Kerry's arm through her sweatshirt.

Kerry likes that she's made Lydia feel embarrassed. Has made things awkward. And then she feels a little ashamed for feeling that way. Growing up, her parents' other favorite expression seemed to be *I'm sorry to say, but* . . . For her and her sisters, it was always the worst "but" clause in the world because whatever happened after that phrase, whatever followed it, was *always* cutting or critical and sometimes mean. But the phrase itself was structured so as to begin with an apology, thereby absolving her mother or father of what followed because they'd begun with *I'm sorry*. Or at least it seemed that was what her parents thought. They'd warned the listener that what they were going to say might be problematic or hard. It almost always was both.

After Kerry's older sister had given birth to her first child, her mother followed "I'm sorry to say" with "but you ate too much and you've ruined your body for good."

"I'm sorry to say," Kerry's father said to her when she

was twenty, "but no one is going to love you if you keep your nail polish chipped up like that all the time."

I'm sorry to say had often been followed by something like *but your friends may not tell you this, and I love you, so I'm going to tell you, hard as it may be to say, hard as it may be to hear.* She wanted to say it now. She wanted to take Lydia's hand in hers, look her in the eye, and say, *I'm sorry to say, but we won't ever be friends. We especially won't be mommy-friends.*

"It's my parents," Kerry says. "My parents are Jamaican."

Lydia looks relieved. A janitor comes in to stack up the chairs, and she tries to follow Lydia's thoughts.

"All you have to do is decorate a table with some things from Jamaica and put up a posterboard with some facts about the island and then have some kind of snack or treat that everyone could taste. I'd help you, of course. If you want."

She watches the janitor watching her. He is trying to figure out if she is a nanny or a mother. This happens all the time in Montclair. She imagines that if she tells Lydia to go fuck herself, the Jamaican booth at International Day will be Lydia sitting next to a TV with an old VHS tape of *Cool Runnings* playing on a loop, a wilted Jamaican flag someone pulled out of a bin on Canal Street poking up from a plastic tablecloth. Who else in this overpriced school is Jamaican? And if she doesn't hand out bite-sized pieces of chicken and beef and vegetable patties, their turmeric-colored pastry flaking all over the floor, who will? There isn't anything funny about why she lives in Upper Montclair.

"Do you need help?" Lydia asks. "You know I went to Jamaica before." Lydia pulls out her cell phone and opens up her Facebook app. "Are we friends on social media?" she asks.

"No. I'm not really on social media," Kerry says. This is true and not true. She has accounts, but she posts nothing. Mostly she uses it to stalk former classmates. But there is definitely no one from Goldenrod on her page.

Lydia opens up an album called "Irie Mon!" and scoots in close to Kerry so that she can see the screen as she scrolls. The pictures are all taken at resorts on the land of her ancestors. She hates that word: *ancestor.* It sounds so practiced, but what else can she call them, honestly? Something like rage bubbles inside her when she sees Lydia posed next to a giant flip-flop, on a boat, choosing mangoes at a roadside market. But what right does she have to be enraged? Kerry is herself what her mother calls *counterfeit Jamaican.* Kerry has never lived there, has never spent more than a consecutive month on the island, always with long stretches in between.

There is Lydia posed under a waterfall. There is a picture of a goat on the dusty, palm-lined street. There is Lydia posed in a jokey Christmas sweater as her family exchanges French press coffeepots and books with images of the Buddha on the cover, perched on a beige veranda, surrounded by other white people, all enjoying the delicious fruits of power.

There are ninety-eight pictures in this album. Ninety-eight pictures of Lydia on a catamaran, of crocodiles on the Black River, of fish-shaped baskets woven from seagrass. Conspicuously absent are Black people. Black people who make up 92 percent of the population. They are nowhere to be found in these photos. Ninety-two percent. But not in Lydia's "Irie Mon" album. In "Irie Mon," the only Black mon is the one who pulls the sails on the catamaran, the one in the background of a rum factory tour, the one bringing things, the one smiling. Smiling. Smiling . . .

"I think I'm good," she says to Lydia. "I have an idea of what to do."

And if they'd ended the conversation there, she would have been safe. Safe to get in the car, to go about her Lydia-hating day. But instead, it continues. Because Lydia is trying so hard, so *desperately* hard to befriend her, and she can't afford to be rude to this woman who controls everything about this school, a place that brings Lady so much pleasure.

It isn't until Lydia pulls out her planner that Kerry realizes she has kind of invited Lydia to dinner. That she has offered to make Jamaican food. She tries to remember how they'd gotten there after her offhand comment about Lady being only a year younger than Lydia's daughter, thinking they might play together sometime. And if she is being truthful, she hopes that Lydia's house might be a place where she can drop Lady off for a few hours, if she needs to get into the city, if Nathan is running late. But somehow, that has morphed into a kind of plan, and all of sudden Lydia, her husband, and their daughter, Pixie, are coming over. She tells Lydia that it will have to be on a Monday. Monday is the only night that works and she hopes that this will make her cancel.

"A school night?" Lydia says, dismayed.

"Sorry," Kerry says. "My schedule is a little crazy." She thinks this is done and that she has extricated herself.

Lydia pulls the cap off her pen. "It's okay," she says, writing Kerry's name into her planner. "It'll be a special treat!"

When Kerry leaves the planning meeting, she calls Nate from the car and tries to explain the dinner invite.

"Well, I'm inviting Pete and Greta, and Alicia and MC, too, then," Nate says.

These are all friends of Nathan's who live in Manhattan and Newark. They are her friends, too . . . kind of. They are not her people, per se. They all talk about books, about movies, which they call *films*. They talk about music she's never heard of. They are obsessed with fusion cuisine.

Finally, Nate says, "Are you there?"

"Yeah. It's just . . . I'm not sure that Lydia and her husband are Pete and Greta and Alicia and MC's kind of people." Kerry pauses for almost too long. "Lydia and her husband might not be as . . ." She searches for the right word. "As cosmopolitan?"

She hopes that if she makes it sound like a question, then it will seem less judgmental than it actually is.

"Exactly," he says. "Exactly."

What she understands about Nathan is that even though these are his friends, these are things he learned. Things he started to understand about New York once he started making money. Once he had some money. He understood that to be Black in America with money meant that these were the kinds of friends he needed to cultivate. The thing he never seemed to forget was space. Nathan had always had this thing about land. He'd never had a backyard, just parks and public space. But Kerry thought that this was what it meant to be a city kid. Yes, you didn't get a yard, but you got muse-ums, and the subway, and Central Park. That was until she realized that Nathan hadn't done those things either growing up.

In Jamaica her grandparents had an acre of snarled

scrubland in the hills outside of Saint Thomas, and
then her parents bought their house in Queens in the
seventies. But Nathan always talked about growing up
in apartments and renting and the way you knew that
the place was both yours and not yours. And when she
was pregnant, he'd touched her belly and looked at her
gently even though she wasn't showing.

"We need a house," he'd said softly. And she laughed
a little bit. Their apartment was the nicest she'd ever
lived in, two bedrooms in Tribeca, better than she'd
ever imagined. Everything was clean and white. Her
parents' house still had rooms of sofas slipcovered in
plastic. The rooms were dark and carpeted and claustro-
phobic, but it was home. But their apartment together
was better than home; it was bright and cool and clean.

"What do we need a house for?"

"For the baby," he said. "I want the baby to have a
yard and a home, a place that they own, that is theirs."

"Babies don't need yards," she said, taking his hands
off her still-flat belly. "I grew up in the city," she said,
taking a box of crackers from the cupboard. "You grew
up in the city."

But they hadn't grown up in the same city, not really. He got cheese for her without asking, like he knew
what she needed.

"You don't grow up here," he said. "You don't get a
childhood; you are just a tiny adult."

He cut the cheese up into small pieces and arranged them in a fan formation on a plate. "You see things," he said. "You see things you shouldn't see."

She thought about this while she ate the cheese and crackers, while she and her belly grew. She thought about it even when they'd signed the mortgage documents, even the first night when Nathan had put his arm around her waist and looked out over the vast expanse of the backyard and he'd said, "It's ours, baby. It's all ours."

By then her stomach was at the point of popping and she'd felt panicked that she would have to make this space and the house behind it theirs.

When Kerry calls her friends in the city to complain about life in Upper Montclair, to complain about how everything is airless and manicured and organized, her friends laugh and ask how she can live there. When Kerry tells stories about Nathan to these friends, he is the kind of husband who cannot remember to sign the permission slip or to get her daughter two matching shoes. The truth is, he is better at these things than Kerry is.

After Lady was born, it seemed right. She was at home during the day, and she did like all the books said and she slept when Lady slept. Nate was back and forth more then, in the city for meetings and dealmaking. Kerry didn't realize she was lucky to be able to sleep until she went to a Mommy and Me group and heard more than one mother laugh at this notion. And they were those angry, barking laughs, the kind without any humor. "And who is going to do the laundry or the cooking or the cleaning?" one said. And another: "My baby doesn't even sleep!" She didn't say anything because Nathan did the laundry, and they ate takeout. And Lady's eyes always seemed heavy with that baby sleep at just about the same time every day. Lucky.

Instead, she calls her mother as she pulls into the Costco in Wayne. Her mother likes when she calls her from the Costco. Kerry knows this. Her mother likes hearing what deals they have. She says it helps her decide whether to make the drive in from the city to buy toilet paper or cod or laundry detergent and, sometimes, to see their granddaughter.

"Hello?" her mother says, sounding as if she has no idea who it is. Kerry knows that when the phone rings her number displays on the television screen and on the phone.

"It's Kerry," she says.

"Oh, Kerry," her mother says. "I guess you remembered you have parents."

It is like every time. They'd spoken just two days earlier, but her parents always do this, make her feel like she neglects them, ignores them. Like she doesn't care about them. On the television in the background, she can hear one of the daytime judges castigating someone in front of the bench.

"Hi, Mummy."

"So, how you doing, baby?" Her voice is softer now. Warm.

Everyone in her family calls her baby, making sure she won't forget that she was the youngest, the one who was different, the only one who left New York, the only one who married a man who wasn't Jamaican.

"I'm good," she says to her mother. "I'm at Costco, buying patties for International Day at Lady's school."

"And what, pray tell, is International Day?"

She describes the event to her mother, who responds simply, "Hmph."

Hmph, that little Jamaican vocal anomaly, the simple and massive judgment of *hmph*, which means many different things, often simultaneously depending on context, including *I wish you were never born.*

"Well, it's a good thing you went to Costco. You can't find a half-decent patty anywhere else nearby."

Her mother thinks Kerry is lucky. Lucky to have what she thinks of as a good life, an easy life in Upper Montclair. For years, Kerry's complained with her sisters about her parents' lack of interest in their lives growing up. This was a running monologue among them, something they'd laughed at over time, about their parents' absence from science fairs and soccer games and school plays, especially when they carted their children to everything from music lessons to meditation retreats. Their parents' refrain had always been the same: *We have to work.* They had to work to afford the house in Queens Village. They had to work to send back money to friends and family on the Island. They had to work so that the girls could do the things they wanted.

But Kerry doesn't have to work. The problem is she doesn't really know what she wants to be doing, but it's not this. But it isn't writing, which also feels fake. Which, if she is honest, she isn't good at either. She pushes her cart up and down the aisles and tells her mother about the accidental dinner party and her promise to make Jamaican food.

"You?" her mother says. "What you know about yard food?" And she laughs, her laugh that sounds like she is trying to hold it in, a *ha ha ha* folded into a cough. It irritates Kerry and makes her homesick at the same time.

Yard food. Food eaten in your yard. Your yard being your home. Yard food being home food. When she was growing up, her mother would always say, *At home, when girls are ten and they don't know how to make a full dinner yet, people will talk.* This comment usually bubbled out in the kitchen, where Kerry and her sisters would be getting lessons on how to season goat or make spinner dumplings to go in the oxtail. She and her sisters knew the kinds of girls her mother was talking about because they regularly heard her on the phone, talking to their aunties about girls like that.

"I don't know what kind of a girl carry on like that—*hmph*—but not my pickney dem. Never!"

The *never* was repeated with such conviction that Kerry was always surprised to visit some of her cousins in Jamaica and taste their overseasoned curry chicken or undercooked rice and peas.

She'd received her first lesson at twelve. Her sisters, already teenagers, were out, their well-crafted lies meant they could have been in Queens Village but just as easily at a house party in Crown Heights or Flatbush.

"When I was growing up, we made the coconut milk from coconuts," her mother had said. She'd started teaching Kerry to make the rice and peas. "But it is so much easier now," she'd said, pulling the Ziploc baggie of coconut milk from the freezer.

Cutting corners or not, the rice and peas still took all day, simmering at low heat on the stove for hours. Kerry would lift the lid every few minutes and watch the beans and rice roll around together in the water.

"Don't touch," her mother said, slapping down the

lid. "Now, the thing you have to remember with rice and peas is that the pepper is the most important part."

Her mother reached into the back of the refrigerator and grabbed an old glass pickle jar, the label mostly peeled off, half full of bright orange and yellow Scotch bonnet peppers, a handful of them, sitting each on top of the other, marinating in their own juices. Just a memory of their intense heat made Kerry's eyes and mouth water.

"The pepper is where all the flavor is. What make the rice and peas taste good. You can't do much to mess up rice and peas," her mother said, spooning in one of the Scotch bonnets. "But careful with the peppers. You burst the pepper, you ruin the rice and peas."

They cooked together, and Kerry imagined her sisters going to their boyfriends' houses, or out to the movies, things their father had forbidden. It was Kerry's job to keep the lies straight. Her mother glanced up at the clock on the wall.

"Now, where are those lazy-lazy sister of yours?" She kissed her teeth and looked at the clock.

"I think they went to Jennifer's house."

As far as Kerry knew, there was no Jennifer. But that was the name she used when she couldn't think of a lie. Her mother thought for a moment.

"Jennifer. Is she the one that came here with no bra on?"

Kerry nodded. She had no idea who her mother was talking about.

"Yes, I remember her now . . . No home training, that girl. No home training. But what you expect from a Trini?"

Her mother laughed at her own joke, doubling over and wiping at the corners of her eyes.

"I guess you don't think that's funny?" she said, looking at Kerry.

Kerry shrugged. She didn't understand her mother's jokes. Briefly, her mother looked like she might explain it to Kerry. But she didn't. She must've thought better of it.

Later that night when they are getting ready for bed, Nathan pops his head around the bathroom door in their master bedroom and asks, "And what's her husband's name again?" Kerry racks her brain. Was it Brian? William? Matthew? She can't remember.

"I think it might be Brian," she says.

"Well, what should I call him?" Nathan asks, poking his head around again.

"Just wait for him to introduce himself," she says. "He will."

Guys like him that she knows love the sound of their own names. She has seen Lydia's husband at school. It seems like he is always pumping someone's hand too hard or clapping someone on the back. He is one of those guys whose voice is so loud that they seem to be starring in a one-man show about themselves, regardless of who is watching.

Monday arrives and twenty minutes before people are meant to arrive, she realizes she forgot to get a bouquet of flowers for the table. At first, she thinks, fuck it, but then she asks Nate to go to the store to get flowers, extra toilet paper for the downstairs bathroom, and a bottle of wine.

"Don't people usually bring wine?" he asks.

"Well, yes," she said, wrapping her hair around a spongy hot curler in the master bathroom. "But you never know. Just go."

On the floor next to her, Lady is pretending to play with a doll but is really watching her.

"Are you doing okay?" she asks, and Lady nods.

"You look pretty," Lady says, and she has her doll nod its felt head in agreement.

Kerry remembers the dinner parties her parents had growing up: heaping pots of curried goat and rice and peas, Jamaican rum punch, and people all over their house late into the night. Bedtime was forgotten, and there were hugs, much too tight, from overly friendly uncles and aunts, tipsy, and beyond tipsy in their basement rumpus room. Not the real relatives. Not the ones who still lived in the house in the hills in Jamaica, but this linkage of other immigrants with whom they shared no blood, but who shared the memories of the Blue Mountains, who had oxtail wrapped in butcher paper in their Deepfreeze instead of Popsicles and French fries, and who kept machetes under their beds. All the things that would keep a body safe in New York.

She pulls out the last of the curlers, and Lady follows her downstairs. She makes place settings and then picks them up again. She can't decide if the dinner will be at the table or if it will be one where everyone ends up crowding into the kitchen for easy access to wine refills and to peer into pots, suspiciously asking, *And what's in that?*

The thought of people looking at the food makes her anxious.

"Can I help you?" Lady asks, and Kerry nods and they reset the table. Just as they finish, Nate comes back with flowers, and wine, and a gallon of ice cream in a clear plastic tub.

"I thought that the kids might like this," he says.

"Ice cream!" Lady shrieks when she sees the tub.

"Not until you've had dinner," Kerry says.

"What's for dinner?" Lady asks.

"Rice and peas," Kerry says. "And curried goat."

Lady wrinkles her nose and clutches her neck like the meal will kill her. And for some reason, it isn't until she sees her daughter perform this gesture that it occurs to Kerry that she should have made something else for the kids. Pizza, or grilled cheese.

"You've had curried goat a million times at your grandparents' house," Kerry says, pulling pots and pans from the fridge. She cooked the entire meal the night before and is going to heat it up on the stove.

"Oh yeah," says Lady, "that's right."

Nathan turns on a video for Lady on his iPad and follows Kerry back upstairs to the bedroom. Kerry likes the way he likes to watch her get dressed. He often does it before she goes into the city. Like Lady, his eyes are big and open. Something about the way he looks at her like this makes her feel prettier, trying on dresses and then dropping them on the floor. Like the way his eyes follow when she adjusts a bra strap or puts on tights from the drawer he's had lined with velvet, just for her. When she's done, Nathan takes her by the wrists and kisses her quick behind the door of their bedroom. And Kerry thinks that he might be the only person who knows her and loves her fully.

The force of the love Nathan's mother had for him scared Kerry sometimes. It was effusive and demonstrative. Each time they visited her, his mother wrapped her arms around him and said, "My baby, my baby, my

baby!" And she looked at him with such joy, such abso-
lute pride, like he'd hung the sun. She was like that with
his brother, Darius, too, the walls of her home almost
sagging under the weight of both boys' pictures, diplo-
mas, and certificates.

"It's like a museum of your life," Kerry said the first
time she visited.

Her own parents' house had only pictures of Jesus
and Colin Powell on the wall. There was hardly any sign
that the two of them had a child or a grandchild between
them. Meanwhile Mrs. Johnson had started a wall dedi-
cated entirely to Lady in her bedroom. Pictures of her as
an infant marched around the door to her bathroom in
a series of small frames, and her kindergarten report card
and a photocopy of her feet at birth flanked the bedside
table.

She hadn't expected such prompt arrival but the doorbell rings at five fifteen and Kerry opens it to see Lydia
and her husband smiling aggressively. She stiff-arms a
bottle of wine at Kerry, who glances over Lydia's shoulder to see Alicia and MC pulling into the driveway. Pete
and Greta had texted a few minutes ago to say they'd hit
traffic but would be there soon.

The other friends—the real friends—had complained about coming over so early. Especially since

Alicia and MC were coming in from the city. Usually when they had them over for dinner, it was right before Lady went to bed and Kerry tucked her in while everyone else started on their first glass of wine and Nate opened a tub of hummus or salsa that he'd picked up at the market. But this isn't going to be that kind of party.

Nate pours wine and mixes cocktails and she serves appetizers in their living room. Pixie and Lady are already up to her room before everyone is settled.

"I want a tour of this gorgeous house," Lydia says.

"Oh, sure," Kerry says.

Behind Lydia's back, Alicia gives her a wide-eyed look like, *Who is this woman?* But the doorbell rings before she can get into it with either of them, and there are Greta and Peter.

Nate takes charge of things, making sure everyone has drinks and offering them some of the cheese and crackers she'd bought at Costco. Kerry goes into the kitchen to lift the lids off the pots. She begrudgingly admits to herself that her mother's trick of making the food the night before makes good sense. The food smells delicious.

When she goes back into the living room, Greta and Peter have commandeered the conversation, discussing their recent contribution to a Haitian NGO. Greta's arguments about NGOs are taken directly from a piece she's heard recently on NPR. There is a heated debate about donating money to organizations like the Red Cross, and Lydia and her husband crouch in the corner. Nate brings Kerry a glass of wine and leans in to whisper something into her ear.

"It's William, but he goes by Billy."

She smiles at Nate. "Dinner should be ready soon," she announces.

Lydia looks relieved.

"I can't wait to try authentic Jamaican food," she says.

"Did anyone see that documentary on PBS last night about Jamaica?" MC asks. He chews on a piece of bread smeared with some of the Spanish cheese. "It was about how the country seems to have fallen apart, since they gained independence in the sixties."

"It was fascinating," Alicia echoes.

Kerry bristles right away. She is the perfect example of assimilation—they all believe this about her—but she can't keep her temper from rising.

"Well," says Nate, "smoking that much herb makes it hard to run a government."

She glares at him, wants to remind him of all the aunties and uncles whose hospitality they have accepted when they are on the Island. In spite of everything—her parents, her set—it's like he forgets sometimes that she isn't just Black like him.

There is a titter of laughter throughout the room,

and she bites the inside of her cheek to keep from snapping at him. She will do that later, behind the door of their oversized bedroom.

Nathan places his hand on the small of her back, like he knows that she is angry, like he is trying to use the hand there to placate her, to tell her that this joke made at her expense is okay. The hand says—he wants it to say—*I don't love you any less. Forgive me. How can I make it right?*

"We went there on our honeymoon," says Greta. "It was beautiful. I paid a little girl on the beach five dollars to braid my hair. Can you imagine? I'd never had my hair braided?"

"That's funny," Kerry says softly. She doesn't realize how flat her voice sounds until she hears herself. She gets up and begins to collect the crush of cocktail napkins. She needs to do something with her hands to keep from smacking that woman in the mouth.

Kerry hadn't realized until she was a teenager—later than she should have—that *some people* almost always meant American people, Black or white. Her parents were so different from her American friends, her lovers, her husband. It was difficult for *some people* to understand the experience of being raised in a Jamaican household while not being in Jamaica. The family, the community, the culture was part of her life. But she wasn't Jamaican, not to Jamaicans. Not to the people she grew up with. To them, she was Black. Just Black. Some people who hadn't grown up eating breakfasts of ackee and saltfish, who hadn't had tablespoons of fish oil every morning, who hadn't swallowed fishy burps all day couldn't understand. There was Blackness, yes. But the cultural experience was too different. The thing holding them together seemed to be skin color and mutual oppression. But everything else felt different. It had been impressed upon her so deeply that she must remember that she was not Black American.

She was different. She thinks about the girl she is writing in the screenplay, the girl who is both her and not her. Every time she tries to give the girl a conflict, nothing comes of it. Her problems are too easily fixable. But easy answers are what audiences want from movies, a friend tells her. She wishes she could write instead about a woman like her, caught between these two things and failing at each. She wishes she could write about that, find a way to put that in a screenplay. Who would watch it? Who would even understand it?

In the kitchen, she checks the food, which is nearly done. She smooths her hand over the newly installed granite countertops and counts to ten. At her grandparents' house, the helper cooks for them. Jerk chicken so hot and so crispy. She knows she can't do that, and her mouth wets with sense memory. She heaps the curry goat and rice and peas into serving dishes and makes child-sized plates for the kids and calls everyone for dinner.

They put the kids in the living room with television trays and turn on *The Princess and the Frog*. In the dining room, they take seats in odd, noncoupled designations, which pushes her to one side of the table, between Pete and Lydia, while William/Billy and Nathan have positioned themselves at each end. Everyone serves themselves, commenting on how good it all smells and looks. In those moments of initial chewing and swallowing, they are all quiet. Silverware scrapes the edges of dishes.

It is Greta who breaks the silence. "But Kerry! This is good."

There is a round robin of agreement, and then the men start talking together across the table.

"Whew," Lydia murmurs. She's seated next to Kerry. "This is spicy! I don't know that I've ever had goat before, but I'm working really hard to be an omnivore."

"Yes," Kerry says, looking in Pete's direction, hoping to engage him in conversation.

"Is Nathan's family from Jamaica, too?" Lydia asks.

"No," Kerry says. "They're American."

"And what does Nathan do for work?"

Kerry has been waiting for this question. She is surprised Lydia has only just now come around to asking

it. They are the only Black family in their neighborhood of stately old homes and driveways with private
gates, Range Rovers and Mercedeses parked in front of
oversized garages. At Goldenrod, there are three other
Black families. They exchange eyes at the events, but
they don't really talk.

"He worked in the music business and created an
app for recording music. He sold that. Did well. Now,
he tries to invest in other Black-owned business."

Lydia's face lights up and Kerry realizes for the first
time that Lydia has clearly had a great deal of Botox.
Kerry is certain that Lydia is older than she is, but there
are none of the telltale lines around her eyes

"That is just fantastic," she says. She takes the tiniest
possible bite of curry goat and leans in closer to Kerry.

"You know," Lydia says, leaning toward her and
dropping her voice. "I went to FAMU."

She leans back and tucks a lock of freshly blow-
dried red hair behind her ear. "You know FAMU, right?
Florida Agricultural and Mechanical University? It's in
Tallahassee, Florida. And it's . . ."—and her voice drops
even lower—"a historically Black college."

Kerry just stares at her and nods. She can't imagine
where this conversation is going.

"I went there to study pharmacy. And man, oh man.
Those Black men were after me. Girl!"

Kerry looks down toward Nate's end of the table,

but he is talking to Greta and MC, gesturing widely, his brow furrowed.

And why is she calling her *girl*? Lydia takes another gulp of her wine. "And you *know* I dated them. Oh yes! Pissed off my daddy properly. But everything I did pissed him off then." She held up a hand, ticking things off on her fingers one by one. "Going to FAMU in the first place; those boys; getting a tattoo; how much I loved DMX. Whew! By the time I dragged Billy's raggedy ass home, they were so happy that he came from a good family that they damn near pushed us to the altar."

Lydia squeezes her arm and smiles at her like she must understand what she is talking about. Again, with the touching.

"Wow."

It's all she can think of to say, because what does this woman want, really?

At the other end of the table, Greta begins a story about the neighbors at the end of their block in Newark. Their neighborhood, midway through a full-fledged gentrification, has made the news for the way young urbanites like them have moved in, rehabbing houses, starting small businesses. Now there is even talk of a high-end coffee chain moving into the area.

"It's like this, you see," Greta says. She is German, and her English is impeccable until she drinks, at which point something old and dark comes out. "The Blacks ruined the area, and now we are here to take it back."

The room is quiet.

"Not you, of course," she says, looking down at her hostess and then back at her host.

Kerry and Nate look at each other, this is something that happens, even among the most well-intentioned of their friends.

"Well, that's rude," Lydia says with a laugh. She puts her napkin down on the table. "You realize," she says, pointing her finger at Greta, "that our hosts are Black, don't you?"

"Wait," Greta says. "Just wait. Let me finish my story."

Lydia lowers her finger and Kerry is both relieved and disappointed.

"There is a house," Greta explains to the table, "at the end of the block . . ."

She describes a lawn full of weeds and a trail of trash leading directly from the garage to the front door. The neighbors themselves are unfriendly and Pete speculates, Greta relates, that they don't work but instead subsist on government assistance.

"Sometimes," Greta says, sipping from a third glass of wine, "sometimes I think I'd like to burn that place to the ground."

"And this is the point of your story?" Lydia says accusatorily. She still manages to smile.

It is Kerry's turn to put her hand on Lydia's arm. To stop her from being the hero.

"Just don't put the gas on your credit card, Greta," Alicia says.

Kerry and Nate exchange another glance. And everyone laughs. Kerry hesitates and then puts a smile on her face. The laughter hurts as much as Greta's words. Because even though this is not the time or the place for a grand white gesture, Kerry is the one who has to restore the equilibrium. Burn a house to the ground? Because they are unneighborly? She pours a third glass of wine for herself. Chews the goat, bites the insides of her cheeks. The goat is tender, cooked in a pressure cooker inherited from her grandmother. But behind the curry, she can taste the slightly metallic tinge of goat flesh, and when she can't chew any longer, she drinks water to move the meat out of her mouth.

"Is there no way for the neighborhood association to buy them out?" William/Billy says.

"Oh, darling," Greta says, waving her fork around. "Newark is urban. Not like this."

"Well," Lydia says, her voice acquiring a sharp edge that Kerry has never heard in it before. "What does that mean?"

Greta shrugs in a way that shows that she doesn't care what Lydia thinks it means.

"Well," Lydia says again, dabbing at her mouth with

the napkin, "I think this is just a great place to live, and I am so glad that Kerry and Nate are a part of our community."

Kerry rolls the word around a little in her mind. What community does she mean? Upper Montclair? Goldenrod? She does not think she belongs at either of these places.

Kerry can feel Lydia's eyes on her but she doesn't meet her gaze. Instead, she looks at Nate, whose eyes flitter a bit. He looks embarrassed.

"Thank you, Lydia," Kerry says. "That means a lot to us. We think this is a great place, too."

"Yes," Nate says in a hollow voice. "A great place."

MC and Alicia smirk at the tone in Nate's voice. These are our friends? Kerry asks herself. Why have they not pushed back against Greta's story? Why haven't they told Greta what the problem was?

Kerry looks down at Lydia's plate. She's surprised at how much Lydia's eaten, the goat gravy completely scraped clean. She'd imagined that Lydia would push the food around her plate, trying to make it look like she'd eaten when she hadn't. Which is what Alicia's plate looks like. So does MC's.

Nate clears away the dishes while Kerry goes to check on the children. Each child occupies a corner of the couch in the playroom—sprawled, relaxed, comfortable. The movie has reached a kind of crescendo, and the cartoon animals sing a big song, kicking across the screen in unison. Both girls' plates are clean, and Kerry takes them into the kitchen and then piles two bowls high with chocolate chip ice cream. Both girls squeal with delight when she puts the dessert in front of them.

Back in the kitchen, she takes her time, feeling no rush to get back to the conversation. To *that* conversation. She finishes another glass of wine, and when she comes back, the party's moved into the living room, all of the dessert plates left on the table.

She sits across from Nathan in an armchair, the too-many glasses of wine making everything look and feel a little hazy. She watches him tells a story about a woman he works with. The story is all buildup to pointing out the funny way his co-worker says Maryland. *Mer-a-land*, like it's inhabited by mermaids. Everyone laughs, and in that moment, she feels almost scared of the way she loves him. Like she could swallow him without chewing, as if he were one of those little pieces of goat meat.

The evening is winding down, although it is not late at all—only seven thirty—but there are children to put to sleep and some people have to drive back to Manhattan . . . Or Newark.

"Thank you so much for having us," Lydia says as

William/Billy helps Pixie into her coat. "I am just so glad we are becoming friends!"

After everyone leaves, and Nathan takes Lady upstairs, Kerry goes into the living room to pick up the sticky ice cream bowls perched on the edges of the coffee table. Kerry is leaning over to reach a napkin wedged under the couch when she gets a strong scent of goat. The meat is piled with the rice and peas inside the pot of a fern next to the window. Kerry knows it was Pixie, knows right down to her marrow that the little girl has scraped the food into the plant.

She pulls the plant into the kitchen and out the back door, throwing the entire thing away. Kerry gets angrier with each step, fuming that Lydia and William/Billy haven't taught their daughter not to do things like this in other people's homes. She thinks about texting Lydia, about telling her that her child has only had ice cream for dinner, that her child wasted food and time, and that her child's decision has probably killed her fern. She wants to be angry at Lydia, and at having to live out here, and at always having her feelings come second to this life of being a mother and a wife. She wants it to be Lydia's fault that she is failing both personally and professionally.

She is back inside now at the sink, scrubbing the scent of soil and plants and curry off her hands when, behind her, she hears, "Mommy?"

Lady is standing there, clean and sweet smelling from her bath.

"My tummy hurts," she says.

And she knows as any parent would that it is Lady and not Pixie who has not eaten the goat.

"Did you eat dinner?" she asks.

Lady smiles slyly. She is not a child prone to guilt. She gets time-outs, not the swats across the bottom or even the face that Kerry got from her parents.

"Not exactly," Lady says. "I took a few bites."

"And what about Pixie? Did she eat hers, or did you both dump them in my plant?"

"No," Lady says. "It was just me. Pixie liked it. She said it was good."

Her parents would have punished her. Would have taken out the leftovers and heated them up right there. Instead, she gives Lady a little ginger ale and makes her a grilled cheese sandwich. Lady is eating it at the kitchen table when Nathan comes down. He is showered and, like Lady, he has that just-washed scent.

"What are you doing up, miss?" he says to Lady. "I thought I put you to bed twenty minutes ago."

"My tummy hurt," Lady says. "Mommy made me a sandwich."

Kerry starts to make one for Nathan, too, who sits next to Lady at the table.

This picture of domesticity, this happy accident. If

only it was all she needed. This life in Upper Montclair. In this moment she looks like a great mother, a perfect mother, but she isn't.

Kerry flips the grilled cheese in the pan and remembers all the lessons she was taught growing up: how to offer an elder tea and biscuits when they come into your home. How to make a bed with tight corners. How to steam wrinkles out of chiffon and silk when drawing a hot bath. How to ensure unwanted guests leave your home by turning a broom upside down and sprinkling it with salt.

In the next few weeks, she will be there in Goldenrod Academy's multipurpose room, like a stand-in for her own mother. She will be Lady's Jamaican mother, handing out bite-sized pieced of chicken and beef and vegetable patties, their turmeric-colored pastry flaking all over the floor where a janitor, maybe even one from Jamaica, will have to clean up the mess. And there isn't anything funny about this. There isn't anything funny about why she lives in Upper Montclair.

She knows her story isn't the immigrant story. It is the one that comes afterward, the one where someone says, *I'm sorry to say but Kerry's parents and grandparents worked hard their whole lives so she could make grilled cheese.*

Some people, Kerry thinks, sliding the plate in front

of Nathan, some people think that work is more important than children.

Is she some people? She doesn't know what is more important than Lady, but something. And she hates herself for it. It is not the dumb screenplay, not her having any professional success, but something. Because one day Lady will be gone, and what will she be left with? She wants to make sure that Lady gets the same lessons she did. But she also wants Lady to reject everything about her.

As she clears away the plates and Nathan takes Lady in his arms, she rewrites the film in her head. The protagonist will not be an ingenue, but a woman in her forties. Her friends will have all moved out of the city and she will find herself caught in endless conversation loops about bake sales or PTA meetings. It won't be funny, it will be sad. She will go out on dates with men who email her gross pictures. Her landlord will offer to reduce her rent if she sleeps with him. She will lose her job, and her cat. She will try to figure out what makes her happy. She will re-create herself until she figures out who she is, asking herself again and again, How did I get here?

The Gifts

HER MOTHER ALWAYS calls England *Foreign*. And when she does, it sounds even better than Peaches can imagine. *Foreign* won't be the tenement yard where they live, or the zinc-roofed market where they buy food, or the men on the corner smelling of overproof rum. In her mind, Foreign is a place where her life will be better, yes, but also where she will be better, too. She won't be like the other girls and women she knows—hair tied up and life tied down with children and men. Girls and women with something missing in their eyes.

When she finally gets to England in the winter of 1960, the days are blustery and cold. She hadn't understood how wind can slip down your neck and into the folds of your dress. Wind—so unlike the breezes she was used to—can catch and cut you when you least expect it. Everything looks different, feels different, sounds different. The cars, the people of every color, shape, and size, it's all different and unexpected. She buys a jacket from the St. Vincent's shop in the Walworth Road where her aunt Tilly told her she'd bought a jacket when she went to Foreign in 1935. Wool and practical, the jacket she finds has a small tag in the lapel that says, *Property of Miss Emmeline Hamill.* All night, she wonders who Miss Hamill is and why she no longer needs this coat.

Her auntie proves an invaluable resource. Peaches gets a job through Miss Jennie, a friend of her aunt's who takes her for a cup of tea in a pub in Coldharbour Lane. Miss Jennie's been in England for almost twenty years now. She wears a felt hat adorned with a clump of red plastic cherries and her shoes are bright red and plastic looking. She doesn't look like any of the women Peaches knows at home. Her hair is pressed and she dresses like the white women in the books that Peaches got at the Salvation Army School.

Even though they are indoors and Peaches is wearing not just her heaviest dress but two pairs of underwear and the thick stockings her uncle sent her from Canada, she is still too cold. She tries to drink the tea as quickly as she can.

"I long to go home," Miss Jennie says, sipping her tea. "I'm too old for all of this anymore. Life in England is always a surprise." She paused, then, "All this time I been here and each day me see something that me never could have imagined in Jamaica."

She adds another sugar to her tea and makes a face after taking a sip. It is early in the afternoon but there are men drinking at the bar. They sound like home, the men—the lilting music of their voices and the way they slap their hands on the bar and laugh.

Miss Jennie looks at them and pinches her mouth. "You'll get used to England," she says. "And then you'll long for home, too."

"Maybe," Peaches says.

Jennie cuts her eyes at her and makes a sound that is halfway between a cough and a laugh. She tells Peaches about a basement flat just down the road here in Brixton, five pounds a week. Then she tells her about the job she's found her in Belgravia.

"This is special," Miss Jennie says. "The Stuarts aren't as fussy as most of the others."

She leans into Peaches and says softly, "Most of the families here would prefer a gyal from Ireland rather than a colored one from the Islands. So behave yourself, you hear?" Miss Jennie sucks her teeth. "You don't have to take up these English ways."

She glares back toward the bar and then returns her eyes to Peaches, looking her up and down, studying her face, her hair, her nails. Miss Jennie thinks she needs washing, styling, and grooming before she is to show

up at the Stuarts in two days' time. Around the corner
from the pub, there is a shop where a woman from her
parish cuts her hair and puts it in drop curls, telling her
to sleep sitting up so she won't muss it. Thankfully it is
Miss Jennie who presses money into the woman's hand
and tells the woman that Peaches is a girl with no one,
and the Lord has told her that she needs to look after
the poor gyal.

So starts Peaches' time in Foreign with new hair
and two new hand-me-down winter dresses from Miss
Jennie's daughters who go to school in Canada. Miss
Jennie presents them to her before she drops her off that
evening at the top of the steps that lead down to her new
cold-water flat.

Everything in the flat feels moist. She stows her
suitcase under the small iron bed and unwraps the thick
brown butcher paper to reveal the two dresses, one plaid
and one dark blue, both freshly pressed. The dresses
smell like soap and something else she can't place. But
they feel like what she wants England to feel like. They
look like they will be the start of her new life.

Wearing Miss Emmeline Hamill's sturdy wool
coat, Peaches takes the Tube into the city very early and
works until it is dark. Mr. and Mrs. Stuart and their
two small children are lovely, and so is their house,
which sits on a street lined with trees. At the end of the
day, she rubs Vaseline into her cracked, dry skin, which

greedily absorbs the salve. She imagines that her life was always like this.

She has been working for them for less than six months when, one damp afternoon, Mr. Stuart meets her in the cloakroom where she is putting on the coat. That coat, the one that she'd thought only months earlier might be too heavy and now seemed much too thin. It never kept her warm no matter how many jumpers she put on underneath. While she's gathering her pocketbook and sliding her feet into the boots she's had to line with cardboard, he suggests dinner, a show. Peaches is too stunned to answer. No man has ever spoken to her this way. It is both exciting and scary.

"Mr. Stuart," she finally manages to say, "I don't think that would be right."

Dropping her eyes, she stares at the intersecting loops, the maze of flowers on the carpet of the cloakroom floor.

"Call me Alistair," he says. She is surprised when he puts his hand on the small of her back and pulls her in close, pressing his lips to hers.

She thinks about that kiss the rest of the evening, and the next day, too, running the moment over and over again in her mind as she takes the children out for air, dresses them for bed, and retreats again to the cloakroom. There, she finds a bundle with her name; inside, a pretty long-sleeved winter dress with paisley print. At nineteen, this is the first gift she has received from a man. And she knows then, somehow, that this is the first, and that there will be more, and that she is only beginning to see what this new life will hold.

At twenty-one, Peaches has become the type of woman who won't demur to gifts. She won't feign modesty or argue that they are too much and then give in to cajoling or pleading. She simply accepts them as they come, when they come, and is grateful.

One winter evening, a package comes as the late-evening sun begins to sink in the sky. The bustle of children coming home from school and men from work has quieted as people take their evening tea. The delivery boy is from Harrods. Harrods deliverymen aren't often in Brixton. Peaches tips five pence. As she shuts the door, she wonders if he was paid extra to come out of central London and cross the Thames.

She pulls the crisp brown paper from the package. Inside are gloves, the ones Peaches saw in the shop window and stopped to admire before Alistair hustled her down the street. She tries them on right away, admires the way her arms look slim and posh in the glass. Long, cashmere, and gray, they come up to her elbows and are fastened by small mother-of-pearl buttons. She puts on the old winter coat; the way the buttons glisten makes the coat look nicer than it is.

She puts the gloves away and reheats a plate of food

the Stuarts' cook has given her. She eats alone, just as she has each night of the two years she's been in England. The food—mushy peas, braised lamb—needs salt. She has never grown accustomed to the food here as she has grown accustomed to so much about life in England. Jamaica feels like a dream sometimes. Even though it's been only two years, the women and men she hears with Jamaican accents in the streets or in Granville Arcade feel like ghosts from another life.

She hears her neighbors moving around in their flats—mothers scolding their children, teenage girls singing along with the radio, the sound of a television set, the smell of fried fish. She has no books, no radio, and no television. She came all the way from Jamaica with one small suitcase. She likes listening to her neighbors in the evening, smelling their cooking while she pretends she is a part of the lives they live.

It is Friday, so tonight she will write her mother, putting in a portion of her weekly wages so that her mother can buy a little extra food, a new dress, a cloth for her table. It isn't much, but there is no one else to give her anything, so Peaches does what she can. When she writes her mother, she tells her about the things that would surprise her—the high-pitched chirp of the train whistle as it pulls into the station, the depth and power of the river Thames, the way the trees bud so lovely in the springtime.

On Saturday, she meets Alistair in Kensington Park and thanks him for the gloves.

"It's nothing," he says. "You wanted them and so they were to be yours."

In the park, he points out all that is new—new buildings, new monuments, to replace everything ruined in the war. The bombs came down, destroying most everything that was old. He tells her he sold books of vouchers to help raise money for the RAF, helped hustle people into air raid shelters, waited patiently for his father to return from Germany. All this, and he was just a boy.

"I'm sure you don't remember any of this," he says. "You would have been just a babe."

"My father," she says quietly. "My father was a British soldier."

He looks at her queerly, taking her hand in his and leading her through narrow pathways shaded by stately greens and foliage-covered squares. They stop when they reach a small cottage tucked toward the Oxford Street gate at the park's western corner.

"This is one of those relics," he says. "One of those things that the Germans didn't get." He lifts the overhanging branches, wiping the glass at the door. Peaches looks in. Like a fairy tale, it is all untouched—covered by a layer of dust, a house left midmorning twenty years prior, when the family ducked into an air raid shelter.

"It's wonderful," she says.

By 1966, Peaches knows of other women like her. It's these women with whom she explores London. They go to restaurants in the high street in Brixton, or to Carnaby Street to peer at the white boys whose hair is as long as the girls' and at the girls with hair cut like boys'. Alistair comes to her, sometimes in the evening, but mostly on Saturdays. He tells his wife he is going to play cards at his club. She makes him oxtail soup and they sit upright in bed, slurping the hot broth. He eats everything, including the marrow, sucking it out of the bones. He asks for more.

"It's good for you," he says, and Peaches fills up his bowl, knowing that his wife doesn't cook for him. She is careful never to bring up his wife, or his children. After he eats, they lie around in bed. There is nothing else to do.

In the six years they've been together, she has learned the way things work. She has traded her dowdy dresses for short printed miniskirts. The boots are no longer lined with cardboard; instead, they are calfskins from a shop in the high street. Instead of going to dances at the Brixton Academy, or the house parties that spiral out from Brixton and Notting Hill and up and up and up into Central London, she stays in. She spends her time with other women like her—those kept, but still working as maids, nannies, and shopgirls—and no one else.

They take tea together in the evening from time to time. But one or the other is always waiting, hoping that she can't make it, that her mister will come strolling down the lane with a tin of biscuits, or wine, or a new dress, or anything that makes her forget that she spends most of her hours alone.

She hasn't seen Miss Jennie in four years. When she'd seen her last, her eyes had taken in Peaches's skirt and the way she wore her hair pressed straight and twisted up at the back of her neck, and it seemed Miss Jennie had understood everything with a glance. She'd sighed softly, and then quietly, almost under her breath, she'd said, "I did warn you about taking up those English ways." Not long after, she stopped trying to get Peaches to go to her church. Stopped inviting her for Sunday supper. Until finally, Peaches stopped hearing from her at all.

Peaches hasn't seen her mother or Jamaica in six years. Her life is watching the Stuart children six days a week, and the evenings and weekends when he comes to her, and that is all.

Peaches comes home the evening of her twenty-fifth birthday. A small portable television sits on the kitchen table. She's never had a television. She plugs it in right away and adjusts the knobs until the fuzzy snowflakes on the screen form into pictures. The knob clicks satisfyingly as she switches between BBC1 and BBC2.

That Saturday, when he comes to her, he pats her head like he would a small child.

"I'm glad you like it, darling," he says. "I couldn't bear the idea of you sitting here each evening on your own."

"I like it very much." She moves toward him and he hugs her lightly, mutters "love you" in her ear, then sits down at the card table and folds his hands together.

"It warms the place up a little, doesn't it?"

"Yes," she says. "It does." Then she puts on the pot to make soup.

It is springtime, her favorite season in London. She likes the way it's rainy and damp but not too cold. But today, it is sunny and the air is cold and clean—a perfect day for a bank holiday. There is something about this time of year that makes her feel really and truly English.

She meets Alistair on the Vauxhall Bridge, halfway between where she lives and where she works. Just last week, when the sun had peeked out again, Peaches took his children to play and picnic on his side of the bridge in Bessborough Gardens.

Peaches left him a note inside his jacket pocket a few days earlier, and so he told his wife he had to work and arranged to meet her here.

"How can you not know how to spell *surely*?" Alistair asks.

He pulls the note out of his pocket and shows her where she misplaced an *h* between the *s* and the *u*.

"I haven't had much schooling," she says.

"I can tell."

She looks away from him and into the muddy river. She is embarrassed then, and the good feelings she'd had just a moment earlier had vanished. Alistair is good at this, making her feel good and bad within seconds. He presses a book into her hands.

"You need to read more," he says. "I had assumed that was how you passed your evenings in that flat, not filling your head with the telly."

"I'm sorry." She watches the Thames, the churning water looking as though it's racing through the city.

"Don't be sorry," he says. "Do better. You have the opportunity of a lifetime living in England. A chance to educate yourself."

The next week the missus tells her they will only need her half-time. The children are in school; there is no need for her to come every day. Her weekly pay packet remains the same, and Alistair enrolls her in night classes—writing and history—and shows her how to take the bus to the adult education center in the financial district.

In her classes she meets other women—some who don't speak English, others who can't read at all. She is the classroom star and the other students are impressed

at her skills, even though she stopped her schooling after grammar school—there was always work to do and
never enough money. But many of the other women, she
learns, didn't even have that much.

She gets a library card, reads books in the evening
while taking her tea. She ignores Alistair's television
and pretty much everything else, falling into sleep on
the narrow metal bed she's slept on each night for the
past seven years.

Alistair quizzes her about her classes, leaves notes in
her pockets with words she must look up in the dictio-
nary. They see each other less and less. She imagines that
he has another Peaches somewhere else in the city. A girl
who is smarter or younger or prettier. She has no one else.

Eventually, she takes a second job cleaning up after
an older woman who lives close to the Stuarts. Peaches
misses him, and still waits for him on evenings when
she doesn't have school—cooking the pots of oxtail
soup, hoping he will come to her soon.

She hasn't seen him in almost a month when he
turns up at her door during the first snowy day of the
season with a stack of books and a request for evening
tea. He doesn't say anything to her until he's eaten.

"I've missed you," he says when he finally comes to her
on the bed and strokes her hair. "Have you missed me?"

"Yes," she says softly. "I was wondering when you'd
come back."

"How is school? Are you enjoying it?"

She brings her books and papers out from the cupboard and spreads them across the bed. She wants him to be proud of her and so she recites the things her teachers have said and tells him about her favorite books, and for a little while he listens. Then he pushes the papers aside.

Though it takes her four years, Peaches completes her secretarial certification. But even so, she cannot imagine leaving her work at the Stuarts. She cannot imagine how she might go and find a job in an office. Who would hire her? These things seem overwhelming. Harder even than getting on the boat that brought her to this country. Weeks will go by when she doesn't hear from Alistair. As the months pass, she grows larger and larger until one day the missus pulls her into the pantry.

"Are you pregnant, girl?"

Almost thirty, she is no longer a girl, which is clear by the way her belly bulges out. She only works for the Stuarts twice a week now, looking after the children when their parents go out in the evening. "I am," she says.

"Well, that's just unacceptable. Totally unacceptable." Mrs. Stuart pulls an envelope out of her pocket and presses it into her hand. "Go. Just go now and don't come back."

Peaches gets on the Tube and begins her ride back to Brixton, trying to imagine how she will manage. She opens the envelope on the train and it is crammed with several hundred pounds of banknotes.

Alistair telephones her in the evening. "I'm going to send you some things," he says.

"And you? When will I see you?"

"Eventually."

The things come, mostly from deliverymen. Peaches tips them what she can, pressing coins into their hands as they set up a crib, a changing table, a wing-backed chair.

When it is time for the baby to come, she calls one of the Jamaican women she has met in her adult education class. The woman arrives with her brother in his car, and they take her to the hospital, where she gives birth to a little boy with curly blond hair and brown eyes. She is there for four days until her friend's brother returns to take her home.

When she opens the door to her flat, Alistair is there, waiting. The flat seems darker, wetter than when she'd left four days earlier, and now it feels like Alistair takes up too much space in it. He takes the baby from her, places him on the bed, unwraps him from the swaddling.

"He's quite lovely."

"Yes," Peaches says. "He is."

She feels like she is about to cry and turns away from him. She puts on the kettle for tea.

"I can't stay," he says. "I won't be taking any tea."

He wraps the baby up, kisses his cheek, and turns toward her. She knows he is there to give her money, she knows she will accept it, and she knows he won't be back.

On an evening in the late winter of 1980, in a chip shop in Paddington, Peaches learns that Alistair has died. She treats herself to fish and chips on Sunday evenings. Fish and chips and the Sunday paper. It is one of the few things she allows herself. She is so tired most of the time that she doesn't have energy for books or friends.

She is at one of the small tables in the chip shop flipping through the paper with one hand and eating with the other when she sees it. The article is buried in the middle of the paper, next to an advertisement for ladies' stockings. She would have missed it had it not been for his picture. She tosses the rest of the fish in the bin and wipes the grease off her fingers. She takes the paper outside and sits on the stoop. She hasn't seen him in almost nine years. Heart failure; his wife found him in bed, cold, his eyes wide open. He'd been the son of a barrister, his family titled; he'd been a barrister himself. The paper talks about a case he'd won in 1971, close to the time their son was born. A landmark British case, the paper said, that had made immigration from the colonies much more difficult. She has trouble understanding the particulars. Suddenly she feels sick. She puts the paper inside her coat and walks toward home.

Sunday is her only day off. She wraps her thin coat tight around her. It is so cold, and she has lost almost two stone this winter alone. It seems there is never enough money, even though she makes much more now, working as a secretary inside an office in central London five days a week and cleaning houses on Saturdays for a little extra.

She hasn't been to Belgravia in years, and she is surprised when she finds herself there. She walks up and down the street, past the house she knew so well, the handle of the front door draped in black bunting. She thinks about crying but can't bring herself round to tears. When she realizes the tears won't come, she gets on the Tube, back to Brixton.

She walks toward home to make her weekly call to her mother and son back on the Island, to tell them things are fine here, to make promises. She will tell her son how much she loves him, how much she misses him; how she will see him soon, even though she has only seen him twice in the eight years since she sent him away. She'll promise him sweets, toys, books, a new pair of flared trousers, any and every gift he wants, gifts she'll wrap in thick brown paper and send to the Island, where his friends will marvel at his fancy mother in Foreign.

Because that is what he calls England, too—Foreign. But he is English. More English than she will ever be. This country is his in ways that he doesn't know yet, but that he will. Because there will be money enough someday to bring him back. Bring him here.

But once she is home, she doesn't pick up the phone right away. In the bathroom, she turns on the faucet and lets it run until the water is clear. She undresses. Too thin now, but her body still looks good, she can say that much. No, she isn't nineteen any longer, she is nearly forty. Maybe the age Miss Jennie was when Peaches came to England?

She gets in the tub, bringing the newspaper with her, running the water at a trickle to keep the bathtub warm. She will be in here a long time tonight. She can't call her boy until she reads about Alistair over and over again. Because someday, maybe soon, he will want to ask about his father. And when that day comes, she will have to decide if she is angry or relieved. She will have to decide if she is going to tell him that this life—her life—was not the better life she'd imagined.

So, she will read until the paper is soggy. Until it melts into the water. She will think about her gifts, the ones that he thinks he gave, and about the ones he really did. But the gift she wants to offer Alistair, for the sake of the boy, is forgiveness. Perhaps that's impossible. But she won't get out until she has separated her feelings from the facts, has asked and answered unspoken questions. She won't get out until the water is cold and her fingers wrinkled. She won't get out and call the boy until she understands what it means to be home.

Waking Life

LAST NIGHT I dreamt of floods. I was being swept away by water and I rode the crest of a large wave trying to escape the crushing force of the flow and trying not to get swept away by the tides. For once I have not dreamt of my mother.

In my waking life I am a writer spending six months doing a series of articles for a travel book about Europe for the twentysomething single girl. I am not twentysomething, and instead of traveling I have spent the past four months falling in love with the German and writing about all the places I am supposed to visit from his Paris loft.

I roll over and look at the clock. It is 6:00 a.m. My alarm won't go off for another forty-five minutes. I hear the steady dripping sound of water on wood, the sound of the rain coming in. This building is old, quaint,

European. The windows leak, the floorboards squeak, and it seems that there are ghosts everywhere. I wonder if there is already a puddle forming on the paint-chipped windowsill. I hope I won't have to clean it up.

I turn back toward Andreas and nestle my body against his. I inhale his scent, deep and musky, a cologne whose name I don't know. But it reminds me of log cabins and winters spent tucked in by snow. He turns to face me, and in his sleep wraps his arm around me and pulls me closer to him. It is a territorial and protective gesture, the kind that usually frightens me in a man.

Andreas mutters something in his native tongue—not the language of his waking life which is a mixture of French and English, mostly for my benefit. The German slips out only in sleep, in fits and bursts and occasionally in nightmares. When he speaks to me during the day, his voice is low, tender. In his dreams the words sound brusque, and I wonder what he says. I wonder what I say in my sleep. My desires? My plans for escape? Or maybe just some fragmentary pieces of my life that I haven't shared with him. That I can't.

I know I hear the water dripping now. "Wake up," I murmur. "Wake up and fix the window." I tug at the blanket and use my finger to trace the shadow of his ribs against his pale white skin and outline the tips of his eyes and the shape of his mouth. My arm is in stark contrast, the brown of my fingers looking almost startling as they trace the fine blond hairs on his stomach. He opens his eyes and looks at me, surprised, and then happy. I love that he always wakes up this way—surprised, and then happy.

"Good morning," he says.

He kisses the tip of my nose. He hugs me and then gets up and pulls the window shut as best as he can. Enough water has leaked in to create a puddle on the floor. He climbs back into bed and he cuddles up next to me, leaving the edges of the bed empty as we both jumble in the middle.

"What time does the train leave?" he asks.

"It leaves at nine thirty from Gare du Nord."

He pretends to sob into his hands. He pantomimes the gesture, trying to lighten the mood. He looks up to see if I am smiling, and I am. "You don't have to go," he says in a high-pitched sniffle and mock-wipes the corners of his eyes with the edge of the pillowcase.

"It's just work," I say. But it isn't and he knows it.

I have never written about London for a guidebook. This will be my first time. I've been assigned a silly series of articles about looking for love in Notting Hill. The insipid movie has inspired my editor to include a rather extended section in the next guidebook series, but this isn't the real work. The real work is seeing the mother who left me when I was three.

"Write from here," he says. He is serious now and

the anger has come to the forefront of his still-blue eyes. "Like you have done with the rest."

I break his gaze and stare at the ceiling. We are on the top floor and I wonder how much insulation there is between us and the water pushing through the rafters and soaking us entirely on the limp platform bed. He has known me for only six months and already he knows how much I want to bolt out into the streets away from him and his love. Or what I think is his love. The idea that he knows this about me is terrifying. I am glad, for a moment, that I will be leaving. Not him, exactly. Just leaving.

"You want to get me fired?" I say, trying to lighten the mood again.

He squeezes my arm and I know he wants me to look him in the eye, because that's the kind of person he is, direct and without apologies. He would never have allowed his mother to leave him. But I get up and empty my dresser drawer. I pull out socks and scarves and stuff them into the backpack wherever they fit. I lay the Ziploc bag containing my grandmother's ashes on top of the neat pile of clothing. I smooth them so they lie flat. "Look at what you're doing," Andreas said. "You are not even packing with sense, you are clearly upset."

I use the weight of my body to squish things into the bulging backpack and zip it up. "I'm not upset."

He holds up his hands in his defense, the cigarette

dangling comically from his lips. "I just want to be there to support you."

"I don't need support." I smile tightly. A smile for school pictures and meeting the mentally disabled. "I'll be fine."

I look around the loft for anything left behind.

"So will you be coming back then?" he says.

I give him the answer I think will make him happy. "I have to," I said, gesturing at my things, a remaining suitcase, a volume of Pablo Neruda poetry, two back issues of *Vogue*, and my hair dryer. I climb into his lap. I didn't want to leave with him being angry at me.

"When you come back, you will stay, yes?" He strokes my hair.

I don't answer. To me, a love affair is something romantic and fleeting. He wants me to live with him in Paris forever. His hair is gray and peeks out in early-morning messiness from the hood of his jacket. "Your backpack is awfully heavy," he says, placing it next to me at the base of the stairs. His tone is suspicious. "Are you sure you won't need assistance with it?"

My granny would have loved him. She always said this was the job of the person who loved you. To help. To protect. My own grandfather had been a shield for her until he'd died. Then she was left, unable to drive a car or even balance a checkbook. But me, I've done too much on my own to require protecting. It would seem silly now.

"I'll be fine. I'll phone."

I reach over and squeeze his arm. He breaks my gaze so I don't see how hurt he really is. It is not only that I do not invite him to come to England, but that I do not want him there.

He leans in and kisses me gently; I keep my eyes open and squeeze him tightly for only a half second. I walk away, and when I reach the end of the block, I turn around and see that he is still standing there watching me go.

I've remembered to take my umbrella. The rain comes down harder and harder. It's the kind of rain that stings, sharp and hard. I step in a puddle and now my shoes and socks are wet. I will squeeze them out in the train bathroom, but they won't really be dry.

I have never gotten soaking wet. My grandmother had never been one for letting a child frolic in the rain. Vanity, which I have in abundance, has not let my meticulously blow-dried hair get wet and has kept me married to an umbrella. Maybe that blow dryer I left with Andreas means more than I think. The ashes in my backpack give me some comfort. My granny did her best to take care of me. Just like Andreas, she always wanted to protect me—shy, frightened, and motherless—from whatever she could. I was so afraid of the dark as a child. Granny rubbed my back each night to help me fall asleep. Her hand would make smooth circles until I fell into the dreams with the rhythms of her voice.

> *Pretty painted butterfly,*
> *What do you do all day,*
> *Fly around the sunny sky,*
> *Nothing to do but play,*
> *Nothing to do but play,*
> *All the livelong day,*
> *Fly butterfly, fly butterfly,*
> *Don't waste your time away.*

I can still hear the notes of the song, soft and musical. Her voice was lilting and took me easily into lush and colorful dreams. Some nights I was that butterfly, soaring, playing, carefree. Other times I couldn't get off the ground. Instead of soaring carefree through the sunny skies, I stayed mired in the image of the woman who had left us both. It was a fuzzy picture. I only vaguely remembered the way she smelled softly and sweetly of the vanilla perfume she must have touched behind her knees before going out.

Soaring like the butterfly is one of the lessons from Granny I didn't pay attention to, but one that comes back to me at night in my dreams. Sometimes I wonder if she really sang it to me or if I just imagined it.

The umbrella gives out on me a block from the train

station. It is blown up by the wind, so I drop it into the nearest trash can and run the rest of the way, pulling up my hood and ducking the raindrops. Having traveled, I know to expect cold springtime showers in Paris. I leave out this detail when I write pieces about springtime in Paris for travel magazines. Those pieces are about having coffee on the Champs-Élysées with a beautiful, light spring breeze blowing your hair about. It is the kind of moment that puts a bounce in a girl's step and a song in her heart. Unfortunately, this is the kind of travel writing I do for a living. It has rained a lot in Paris lately; a cloudy March has turned into a rainy April, and the rain has become increasingly cold, damp, and uninviting.

I call my mother from the railway station. Our meeting was arranged a year earlier, after a condolence card came, my name on the front in slanting backward script. *Warmest regards on the death of your mother* and her signature dashed hastily inside. But there was no phone call. I'd waited for days to hear her voice crackle long distance over the telephone line. But it never came. I had Granny cremated and was humbled when they handed me the tiny box at the funeral home. She was a small woman, but I still expected there to be something more substantial in her ashes. There is no heft to ashes. It was sad to think that this was all that Granny was made up of.

So I'd called my mother and got a rushed invitation

to "pop round if I was in London." I had hidden from her for months in France before a deadline had forced the issue.

The trains rumble in the background, and efficient, textbook French calls out the train platforms.

"Londre, Voie B. Londre, Voie B."

It is my train they are calling. I pull out the crumpled card. I got the number months ago from an overseas operator. I make sure I push each button carefully. The telephone rings and rings. I reach her answerphone and the message is bright and chipper.

"Hullo, you've reached Janice and I'm afraid I'm engaged at the moment but leave a message and I'll return your call."

My stomach turns and I want to hang up. I wait for the beep.

"Yes, hi, it's Po, ah, Pauline. I'm just calling to confirm that I'll meet you at Prince Albert pub in Coldharbour Lane at six."

I hang up quickly and head toward my track.

Trains leave the station hourly. They go everywhere and anywhere. The click of the schedule board in the train station whips through cities every few minutes: Amsterdam, Marseille, London, Toulouse, Dijon. The trains shoot off into the outer edges of Paris, all abandoned railroad cars with French graffiti and highrise apartment buildings. The train shuffles out past industrial complexes until it suddenly goes through a tunnel and comes out the other end in a different France. This France, unlike the one with the high-rises, is the one that waxes poetic, fields of sunflowers, lavender as you go farther north, cottages with red-tiled roofs, and sun that lights up the faces of freshly scrubbed French children as the train whips through their town. I fall asleep, my mouth open, the drool puddling on my bottom lip.

I dream of my mother. Her small house, its thatched roof, and there are children playing in the front garden. A little girl and a little boy with curly brown hair who smile when they see me.

"Po!" they call out, and run up and grab me by the legs and I hug them and I am so happy. I kiss their fat little cheeks and we go into the house together. There are biscuits with honey and tea and my mother greets me with a smile and kisses me on both cheeks.

"We've been waiting for you, Po."

She calls me Po, my grandmother's pet name for me, and strokes my hair and tells me how lovely I have become.

She is beautiful, her hair is long and shiny, her face is round, warm, and welcoming. We sit and talk. The clock strikes three and she looks up, worried.

"You have to go, Po," she says.

"But Mummy, I just got here. Can't I stay?"

She laughs a tinkling and lilting laugh and grabs my arm and squeezes it.

"No, Po, you don't belong here. This is my life, darlin', not yours."

Her grip on my arm becomes tighter as she guides me toward the door. I wake up and tears are on my cheeks. The dreams are so vivid I wake up with a five-year-old's desire for mummy. I stretch out and check that my backpack is under my seat, that Granny is still safe. In my dreams I find my mother and the reunion is always beautiful. She welcomes me into her arms with a Crest-toothpaste smile and apologizes to me for every single second we've ever spent apart.

The countryside whips past me now in a blur of images. The flowers, the hills, the cottages. I have not been out in the French countryside in a long time, and on this particular trip I have yet to leave Paris. I rub my eyes and stretch. There is a tiny French girl sitting across from me. Her body is small, but she has a large head and big green eyes. Her curly hair is done up in pigtails. She twists her hair with one hand and eats with the other.

"Bonjour, Mademoiselle," she says, then takes a bite out of a baguette, nearly her size, slathered with butter and jam.

She looks too small to be riding the train alone and I don't see her family anywhere around. The car is half empty. Passengers drift in and out, students traveling in groups, business travelers sipping coffee from the dining car.

"Avez-vous faim?" The little girl holds out her bread, offering me a piece, I shake my head no. The little girl shrugs and gets up, smearing jam on the armrest. She walks out of the car. As she leaves I realize I should have helped her find her parents, asked her name, or found a conductor to look after her. I can't imagine what kind of mother I would be. Perhaps the type that would let a small child wander around a train full of people alone.

I close my eyes and I plan out the rest of the trip. Once I get to London, I will check in to my hotel, and I will make my way into Brixton. Other tour books have described the place as having "palpable Caribbean flavor."

The cabin door slams open and a heavy older woman walks into the car. Her hair is tied back with a scarf printed with brightly colored blue and red parrots, their tails create a fan down her back. Gray hair peeks out under her scarf at the temples. She wears a clashing light pink windbreaker over an orange-print T-shirt. Her eyes dart quickly around the cabin.

"Bernice," she calls out. "Bernice!? Don't you hear when your granny call you?"

The last part is delivered frantically and I recognize the same frenetic Jamaican patois that my grandmother always used when she would try to find me on the playground. I would hide and pretend I didn't know her. I would pretend that it wasn't my name that she called.

"Po!" my grandmother would call, her head tied in that hair scarf I hated, her house slippers dirtied with the dust of the playground's small, pebbled surface. "Don't you hear when Granny call you?"

I feel ashamed for all the moments that I screamed at my grandmother, "You are not my mother and I hate you." For the times I told the kids in middle school that she was not my grandmother, but my babysitter. She had been the only person to look after me, and I was too rushed to pretend I wasn't upset by her death, that I hadn't even given her the funeral she deserved for that effort. I haven't been nice. But I will make things up with my mother.

The woman calls one more time and looks around the car. I look away because sometimes you see people from the Island and they want to know you. They want to play: *Who your parents? Where they from? What you doing all alone in Foreign?* I watch the French countryside whip by my window as we near the Chunnel. I do not want to be peppered with questions for which I have no answers while submerged under thousands of feet of water, trapped.

We go underground and there is darkness, and in the window's reflection, I see the woman standing behind me in the aisle looking out the opposite window, gazing into the dark and shifting her weight from one foot to another. She looks lost, staring at her own reflection. I wonder what she sees, if she is trying to figure out how she got here.

The little girl wanders back into the cabin. The bread is gone and her face is dirty.

"Grand-mère!" she says, surprised to see the woman standing in the aisle. She climbs into the woman's arms, puts her little arms around her neck, and kisses the woman's face. This is Bernice. The woman nods and pats the little girl. She strokes the child's hair roughly and lets herself be kissed. She looks out the window again into the darkness and I think maybe she can see something I can't.

After I check in to my hotel, I spend the early afternoon going to Harrods and browsing in the shops on Oxford Street. I find young women to talk to for my article. I pretend to look for places to pick up eligible Englishmen. The city seems to be crawling with Jamaicans. I imagine what Brixton will be like. I stop in Selfridges and buy a tin of sweets for my mother filled with assorted biscuits, jellies, shortbreads, and chocolates.

The store is thick with tourists looking for afternoon tea and I stop into one of the telephone boxes and dial Andreas's number. He answers after the second ring.

"Allo."

"Hello, it's me."

"Hello, chou."

It is reassuring to hear his voice again and I close my eyes and let it slide over me.

"How is London?"

"All right. It's overcast here. I suspect it's going to rain soon."

Our conversation is forced and stilted over the telephone. What am I thinking? Of course I cannot go back to this man, not for the long term, perhaps not even for the short term. I think about taking the Tube out to Heathrow and charging a ticket to New York on my credit card.

"Well, try not to get too wet. I wouldn't want you to catch cold," he says.

There is a pause and I try to think of something to say that will not give this phone call unexpected weight.

"I miss you," he says finally.

"I know."

"When are you coming back?"

"I don't know," I say. "It is hard for me to tell how long things will take here."

"No excuse please, Po. Just come back."

His voice is intense, serious. There will be no overly romantic gestures or pleas, just a simple request to come back and give things a chance with him.

"Yeah," I say. "I'm still thinking."

I look at my watch. I will get on the Tube soon and ride down to Brixton.

"What is to think about? I love you," he says.

"Me too," I say breezily, and place the phone back in its cradle.

I put the tin of biscuits in my backpack and head back out into the street where it is overcast and gray.

Brixton is not the London that tourists often see. The fanny packs, sprawling maps, and newly white sneakers all but disappear as the Victoria Line chugs toward Brixton. As we move farther and farther from the city center, the train stops less frequently. The ride between the Vauxhall and the Brixton stations seems interminable. A pleasantly accented voice informs us that this is the end of the line as the train pulls into the station.

It is not raining yet in Brixton, but the sky is dark and I can see the potential forming in the ominous clouds. I am not meeting my mother for another hour. I wander up Electric Avenue where the Tube has left me. I remember the song with a smile. I'd read once in an old issue of *NME* that Eddy Grant had written the song about the lack of acknowledgment of Brixton's growing Caribbean population. This is my mother's home, and in her neighborhood I feel as confused as ever.

I am one of a long tradition of Jamaican children left behind by their parents. They go off to Canada, to the United States, to England, and then they send for us when the money is good, when the weather is warm, when they have found a school where they can bully the teachers. My mother left me in Toronto, in the middle of the winter. I was born there, and sometime before my second birthday, my mother's husband—my father—disappeared, and so Granny came to stay. My mother was young and inexperienced, or so Granny told me. I heard stories about my diapers being put on backward and my mother letting me run around the house naked whenever my little heart desired. These stories would make Granny laugh until the tears at the corners of her eyes turned to the kind that come from sadness instead of happiness, and then she would get quiet and say Mummy's name and sigh. When I was three and my mother decided to move to England, I was left with Granny.

The Brixton Market on Electric Avenue is bustling. I walk through stalls with halal meats and consignment clothing. It reminds me of the Portobello Road Market, but I remember I am at the outskirts of London and I am surrounded not by overzealous tourists but neighborhood people doing their shopping. I fantasize about my mother rummaging though the stalls, picking out breadfruits and ackee for a Sunday brunch. There is no need to take notes here.

There are still another forty-five minutes before I meet my mother. The pub is on this street, the Prince

Albert—her choice, not mine. I had never ventured into
Brixton during any of my previous trips to London. I
walked the areas that my industry traffics in: Big Ben,
Westminster Abbey, Buckingham Palace. Travel writers
don't enjoy the travel so much as describe the mundane
details—places you can use your student ID, where to
go for a cheap lunch, and sadly, in my case, where to
meet other cute backpackers.

I never much enjoyed traveling in London. The idea
of my mother has always hung over the city, like the
ghosts that supposedly haunt some of London's most fa-
mous monuments. I could always feel the specter of her
hanging over the city. But there has never been a need
to find her before now. My grandmother was alive then,
and I didn't want a mother who did not want me. In the
past Granny suggested seeing her, slipping my mother's
number in my purse and awaiting my arrival from each
trip to the UK with a breathless anticipation. But she
didn't ask, I think, mostly because she didn't want me
to know how much she cared.

The streetlights are coming on now and the sun
lowers and seems to want to hang for a moment before
dipping out of sight. I have been warned about Brixton at night, its muggers and drug dealers. But I think
that it looks much safer than Alphabet City, the rough
edges of the East Village where I live. A bit of sunlight
peeks through the clouds and hits a metal sign across

the street, illuminating the word *Joy*. The letters sparkle in their last bit of the late-evening sunlight and I shield my eyes from the glare. My arms goose pimple and I look right, then left, and then sprint quickly across the street and pull open the shop doors.

The shop is crammed with bits of jewelry and hip clothing, trousers with *Black Sabbath* stenciled across the bottoms and T-shirts with anachronistic screen printings. It is the type of shop I would have loved when I was twenty. I flip through stacks of books about Elvis, detox, Botox, and yoga. I browse dishes with *eat* painted on them and backpacks crafted from refuse. During my months with Andreas, I have broken six of his wineglasses. I pick out two with delicate stems and hand-painted globes. They are tacky. But I want to replace the broken ones.

The saleslady wraps the glasses in confetti-colored tissue paper and I tuck them inside my backpack. I look at my watch. I have another five minutes to kill. I wonder if this shop has brought anyone the sentiment that is its intent. I want to walk out feeling light and happy, like the kitschy pictures and novelty T-shirts advise.

I have forgotten that people in London begin drinking early in the day. The Prince Albert is more than half full by the time I reach it.

I don't know if I will remember what my mother looks like, so I scan the crowd for a dark face that looks familiar. There are none, so I sit at a table near the window. I get a cup of tea. She is late. The rain has started and fat drops hit the glass with a steady beat. Even now I begin to fantasize about my mother's lateness. I daydream that she is buying me a gift. I think that she is rushing to pick up a husband who she cannot wait for me to meet.

My backpack is large and I wedge it beneath my seat. It is large enough to hold the biscuits and the wineglasses and a piece of Granny. This is the part of Granny I brought for my mother. This will be our connection. Granny will bring us close, the way she never could in her life. We will have one of those Lifetime-channel-movie moments where we're both so achingly beautiful, sad, and touching that you cannot help but fall in love with both of us.

She is twenty minutes late now and my panic begins to set in when the door swings open. I am surprised. She looks young. Her hair is cropped close to her head and is tapered expertly at the back of her neck. Her jewelry is tasteful and stylish. She is slightly overweight, but still looks like a career-minded, savvy woman, not the kind that you would think had a thirty-year-old daughter dressed in wrinkled jeans who lives more than half the year out of luggage. She wears the kind of sunglasses that wrap around, covering even her peripheral vision. They are both costumey and chic. She comes right toward me. I get up to greet her.

"Pauline." She hugs me lightly, patting my back in a way that reminds me not to linger too long. Three quick pats and she releases me without sentiment.

"It's Po," I say. "Everyone calls me 'Po' instead of Pauline."

"Well, yes, I see."

There is none of the music in her voice that was in my grandmother's. Her tone is flat. British inflections have mellowed the Jamaican musicality. She studies me through the shades and I wonder why she doesn't take them off.

"So, Po, is it? Would you be a darling and get me a pint at the bar."

I get up to get the glass without even a *please* from her, trying so hard to be the obedient daughter. When I come back she has taken off her sunglasses and is cleaning them with a napkin. I set the glass down in front of her and she pats my hand lightly as a thank-you.

"So how did you choose an odd little name like *Po*?" she asks, setting the sunglasses down.

"Granny said that *Pauline* was too much of a name for a little girl, so she called me Popo, and then as I got older, just Po."

It seems odd explaining a name I've had as long as

I can remember to the woman who gave birth to me. She laughs, but it's not the laugh from my dreams. My mother's laugh is harsh, the sound of pebbles being thrown against a metal garage door.

"Well, that's lovely, dear. It was so kind of you to think of me while you were here. What is it you do again, darling?"

She takes a sip of the ale, and I explain the travel writing, the books about backpacking, European vacations for the single girl. I am tap-dancing, doing jazz hands, cartwheeling, and doing my best to scream out *love me, love me, love me!* As I speak, I realize I don't know what she does. When I finish, she looks at me curiously.

"What an odd job. And you enjoy this, do you?"

I am flustered.

"Yes. Yes, I guess I do. It's challenging, interesting, lots of opportunities."

"Odd," she says again, leaning back into her seat. "Quite odd."

She gets quiet and I wait for the glowing woman of my dreams. I wait for her to tell me how much she loves me, how sorry she is, how she missed me. But instead she begins to talk about Granny.

"I was sorry to hear about your granny," she says, as though she had no connection to the woman. "But I'm not surprised. That woman did absolutely nothing for herself but was always putting herself out for other people."

I don't know what to say.

"She did a lot for me, but I won't ever live my life that way," Janice continues, taking a sip from the ale. "If you learn one thing, Po, learn that you can't live for anyone but yourself." She leans across the table. "Always make yourself the priority."

I feel the anger rise up into my face and I hold myself back.

"I think Granny always wanted to make sure everyone was taken care of. I think that made her happy, to make sure that people got the things they needed. She certainly made sure that I always had the things I needed or wanted."

She seems oblivious and shrugs her shoulders.

"Well, hope you don't end up like her," Janice says. "I think I'm a much better role model in that department. Besides, you don't know everything about your granny."

I lean back in my chair and wonder how she can say this to me.

"What can you tell me that I don't already know about her?"

I keep my tone even.

"She was judgmental as all hell," my mother says. She begins systematically tearing a napkin to shreds, one of my own nervous habits. "You couldn't do one thing wrong without that woman holding it over your head for the rest of your bloody life."

This is not what I know of my Granny.

"She tried to make everything a parable, a lesson to be learned, and sometimes I just wanted to say, 'Okay, okay. I fucked it up proper and I know that. You don't have to couch it in some sort of moral high ground.' She could never say anything directly, it was always about a song, or an Anansi story. Bloody hell. I hated listening to her go on and on about what was right, as though her way was the only right way."

Janice has raised her voice to a near-shouting pitch and a couple at the next table looks over at us and she glares at them with a sense of entitlement. These are all the things I loved about my granny, the gentleness, the way she let me figure things out for myself. Janice grabs my hand and I look into her eyes for the first time. They are cold and it takes me a while, but I realize that she has clearly been drinking for hours.

"I hope you didn't let her brainwash you against me. I am. A. Good person."

Her grip on my hand is tight and when she lets go of my fingers, they are red and the blood rushes back into the digits gratefully. She has been drinking more than the ale she has been sipping for the past half hour. Not just one glass of wine, but the kind of drinking that has made her eyes bloodshot and her hands shaky as she reaches for the glass on the table in front of her.

"Well, why did you leave then?" I say it quietly because asking the question terrifies me and I know I will have to hear an answer and live with whatever it is. No more dreams.

She shrugs her shoulders at my question. My stomach bottoms out around my feet and she smiles at me with a tight-lipped smile that is so fake and repellent that I want to smack the glass from her hand.

"I was young," she says. "Besides, your granny was better at mothering. I never really liked it. I never really wanted to have children. You see, I work in fashion now," she says with a look that seems to want me to be proud of her. "I manage a textile company. You see, I wanted to be more than just a mother."

She looks at me pityingly, as though she is explaining this to a small child, who cannot understand the importance of a career or success. Mothering, she is telling me, was less important than textiles. My head swims and I don't know what to say. Did she get drunk because she was frightened of me? Because she knew my questions would be too hard and she needed to shield their blow? Or is my mother just a drunk? I don't know and I don't care enough to ask. We finish our drinks and she slips her sunglasses back on. It is raining harder and harder. Without the umbrella I will be soaked.

In the window I see people shielding their faces against the rain. The wind whips and shrieks louder and louder as a woman's umbrella is blown inside out. I lean over, reaching under my seat and unzipping the backpack without taking it out. Inside, my hand finds the tin of sweets and the edges of the Ziploc bag. I think about giving Granny to this woman, but what connection will she have to either of us? I imagine Janice stuffing the Ziploc in the back seat of her car and forgetting about it, or tucking it into her garage behind a pair of hedge clippers. She would throw Granny away the same way she had thrown me away. I pull the zipper closed and straighten up.

"Is there something else I can do for you, dear? I do have some other errands to do tonight."

"No," I say. "I just thought it was important that we meet."

"Yes," she says with a confused frown. "Yes, I guess it is, family and such. We can chat another time I suppose. Can I give you a ride somewhere?"

I refuse and she gathers her expensive pocketbook and pulls on her jacket. The hug is another quick three pats on the back.

"Well, give me a ring next time you're in the city and we'll chat or something, love."

I watch her go out into the gusty evening rain. I sit there for an hour. I have another cup of tea. I think about my grandmother in my backpack. I don't know what to do with the piece of her that belongs to my mother. The ashes are all I have left now of a family. I know I will never see my mother again. I won't write or call, she will probably change her telephone number.

I stay in the Prince Albert pub until the rain begins to let up. The streets of Brixton are quiet in the early evening and most of the shops are in the process of shutting their doors. It is a weeknight and I imagine people will head back home to families that love them. I have no one to go to. But I did for a little while, didn't I? I think about Andreas. Can a person will a home into being? Call it forth?

I go out into the drizzle and catch a cab back into Central London. I have done what my grandmother would have wanted. I tried to make amends, but the certainty of my mother's rejection floors me. Soon, the shock of realizing that I have rejected her, too, brings hot, stinging tears to my eyes.

"Let me out here," I say to the cabdriver as we cross over Westminster Bridge. I get out in front of the Abbey and I watch as tourists line up for the final tour of the day.

The Abbey is haunted with ghosts and I am among them. I see myself visiting the Abbey for the first time at eighteen, hoping in vain to see my mother somewhere in London's crowded throngs of people, but too frightened to seek her out. But I've done that now and I am sorry. I turn away and walk toward the clock tower. The rain begins coming down hard and I am without an umbrella. I'm dressed up to see my mother—a skirt, leather kitten-heeled boots, and an expensive children's T-shirt from Petit Bateau that cost a month's worth of pay. It doesn't matter. None of it mattered.

The clock chimes for 8:00 p.m. and on the banks of the Thames, the rain hits my cheeks. It feels calming. Granny has never been one to keep a grudge. Forgive and forget, she said again and again. I could not recall ever having felt the rain beat down upon me. It makes me sad that I have had to wait until I am thirty to experience this for the first time. The water of the Thames is rough. It has seen centuries of turmoil itself. I look up to the London Eye, a maniacal Ferris wheel rising to look out over the city. It can see me, here on the banks of the river, sad and disappointed. I wonder if it sees my mother, wherever she is, in the heart of Brixton, shopping on the high street, spending time with some family, in some life that I can't touch or try to become a part of.

My grandmother's ashes are still with me. I wonder if she is proud of me. Even with my silly career and my erratic love life, I wonder if she wants to make sure that there is a part of me that is happy, a part that is loved, a part that is protected.

If there is a heaven, I hope she is there. I pull off

my backpack, unzipping it and searching for the sweets. I touch the fine tissue paper and I realize the glasses are shattered. I pull them out of my bag and shake the glass out into my hand. The fine slivers are colorful and bright. I throw them into the Thames. I pry open the lid of the tin from Selfridges and eat everything in it, sitting alone as the rain soaks through me.

I want to think that water can wash away all things. The piece that I have of my grandmother wants me to remember, though. The water will not wash us away from each other.

I walk up through the city. When I get back to my hotel, I drip water on the expensive carpets and I don't care. Rivulets of mascara have run down my cheeks and I look frightening. I had wanted so badly to look pretty. I use the house phone to call Andreas. I get the answering machine with him greeting me in both German and French; it sounds a lot like love. I leave him a message in English. I want it to be cooing and lovely. Instead, it is simple.

"Tomorrow."

Acknowledgments

I am humbled and honored to have worked with Leigh Newman, who has helped this collection sing. Who with grace, kindness, and patience worked with me to make these stories a truer reflection of the people and places that color my imagination.

To my family: George and Maxine Kelly, Jay and Sara Bremyer, Adrienne Wallace, Simone Kelly, Anton Kelly, Keisha Kelly-Thompson, Kris Kelly, Seth Bremyer, Camille Kelly, John Thompson, Logan Wallace, Rhys and Tristan Kelly, Izadora Wallace, and Janice Bent. And my late uncle Ian. Thank you always for your love, patience, confidence, and support.

For the friends new, old, and enduring who have supported me over the years; reading, writing, and showing up with love: Carrie Ismail, Pam Sutton, Kristen

Chernosky, Carrie Hall, Kimberly Mock Nielson, Kathe Roper, Karen Gentry, Emily Weekley, Chelsea Rathburn, Jim May, Chad and Gwen Davidson, Kelcey Ervick, Margaret Mitchell, Charlotte Pence, Karen Lee Boren, Wally Lamb, Alison Umminger, Mike Mattison, Greg and Milada Fraser, Meg Pearson, Marcus Marenda, Jade Loicano, Ann Marie and Ed Short, Jamie and Jake Wagman, Stacy Davis, Teri Suico, Natasha Walker, Laura Beasley, Jake Mattox, Laura Ambrose, Krista Hoefle, Bettina Spencer, Adam Prince, E. J. Levy, Robert Long Foreman, Perin Gurel, C. J. Hauser, Nafissa Thompson-Spires, Avni Vyas, Azareen Van Der Vilet Oloomi, Calaya Stallworth, Joyce Wilson, Amina Gautier, Hasanthika Sirisena, Sal Peralta, Pam Murphy, Muriel Cormican, Kevin Casper, Michael Nye, Jason Myers, Laurah Norton, Josh Russell, Elizabeth Stuckey-French, Brian and Kathleen Powers.

For support I have received for these stories from Evelyn Somers, the Voice of Our Nations Arts Foundation, the Sewanee Writers Conference, the Newnan Art Residency, Saint Mary's College, the University of West Georgia, and the University of Notre Dame.

To my two most favorite people on the planet, Ellison and Aaron, thank you for making me laugh, for loving me as I am, for supporting me. Ellison, this book is because of you, and for you. And Aaron, without whom none of this is possible, for all that you give, for all that you do, for who you are . . . it won't ever be enough but thank you.

© Myriam Nicodemus

DIONNE IRVING is originally from Toronto, Ontario. Her work has appeared in *Story*, *Boulevard*, *Literary Hub*, *The Missouri Review*, and *New Delta Review*, among other journals and magazines. Her first novel, *Quint*, came out in the fall of 2021. She currently teaches in the creative writing program and the Initiative on Race and Resilience at the University of Notre Dame. She lives in Indiana with her husband and son.